THE DISGRACEFUL DUKE

Shimona was face to face with the notorious Duke. She had imagined an older man with slanting eyes, arched eyebrows, a long thin nose and pointed ears.

But as she looked across the room she saw not the devil she had anticipated, but a surprisingly young, extremely good-looking man.

He looked at her with an expression that made her body tremble and her heart pound wildly.

Appalled by her own ecstasy, she blushed and turned from the Duke's penetrating gaze.

BARBARA CARTLAND

Bantam Books by Barbara Cartland
Ask your bookseller for the books you have missed

Barbara Cartland
The Disgraceful Duke

BANTAM BOOKS
TORONTO · NEW YORK · LONDON

THE DISGRACEFUL DUKE
A Bantam Book | February 1977

ISBN 0–553–10340–7

Published simultaneously in the United States and Canada

Bantam Books are published by Bantam Books, Inc. Its trade-
mark consisting of the words "Bantam Books" and the por-
trayal of a bantam, is registered in the United States Patent
Office and in other countries. Marca Registrada. Bantam
Books, Inc., 666 Fifth Avenue, New York, New York 10019.

PRINTED IN THE UNITED STATES OF AMERICA

Author's Note

The Theatre Royal, Drury Lane, continued to be unlucky until 1809, when it was destroyed by fire—the blaze lit all London.

Richard Brinsley Sheridan was faced with utter ruin, as the building was under-insured.

The theatre was rebuilt and opened in October 1811, and is the Drury Lane we know today. It is the theatre of Edward Kean—the greatest Shylock of all time—of Elliston, Macready, Dan Leno, Sir Johnstone Forbes-Robertson, and Sir Henry Irving.

From Nell Gwynne to Ivor Novello, Drury Lane stands alone; no other city in the world has its rival.

It is part of our history and as long as London lasts there will always be a part of it known as the Theatre Royal, Drury Lane.

Chapter One

1803

"How do you feel, Papa?"

"I will—be all—right," Beau Bardsley gasped.

But as he spoke he sank down on his chair in the dressing-room and stared at his face in the mirror with an expression almost of despair.

Shimona hovered behind him, uncertain what she should do.

The fit of coughing which had racked her father in the passage after they had entered the stage-door seemed to have sapped his strength to the point of exhaustion.

Without speaking, Joe Hewitt—Beau Bardsley's dresser—brought his master a glass of brandy mixed with water, and set it down on the dressing-table beside the grease-paint, the salves, the powder-puffs, and the hare's foot.

To lift it to his lips Beau Bardsley had to employ both hands.

After a few sips the spirit seemed to revive him and in a very different voice he said to his daughter:

"You should not have come here with me."

"I do not intend to leave you, Papa," Shimona replied firmly. "You know as well as I do that you ought not to be performing today."

Beau Bardsley did not reply and they both knew the answer without having to put it into words.

He had to work.

Not only did he require his salary to keep them

1

alive, but it was also only a question of a week or so
before the management of the Theatre Royal, Drury
Lane, would consider him due for a benefit.

Beau Bardsley drew his watch from his waist-coat
pocket with a shaking hand.

"You've plenty of time, Mr. Bardsley," Joe Hewitt
said in a soothing tone, as if he fancied his master was
worrying about it.

Beau Bardsley gave a deep sigh.

They all knew that in his present state it would
require considerable physical effort on his part to get
into the clothes he wore as Hamlet.

There was one blessing, however, Shimona thought
to herself.

Her father had played the part so often that it was
no effort for him to remember his lines, and once he
faced the footlights he would be inspired as he always
was by the applause and adulation of his admirers.

At the same time, the Theatre Royal, Drury Lane,
was filling up with an audience who acclaimed Beau
Bardsley as one of the finest actors Old Drury had ever
known.

They came to see him even though at the moment
the theatre itself had fallen on hard times.

Mrs. Sarah Siddons, who had reigned there as the
undisputed Queen for twenty-one years, had left London to rest. When she returned, it was to the stage at
Covent Garden.

There was an almost insurmountable difficulty in
finding an actress capable of taking her place.

But as long as Beau Bardsley was billed, the audience flocked in. Unfortunately, his health often prevented him from honouring his commitments.

He put out his hand now to pick up the grease-
stick and as he did so he could see Shimona reflected in
the mirror.

"You should not have come here," he said again.
"You know I do not allow you to be seen in the theatre."

"Joe can keep your visitors away," Shimona replied with a smile. "Besides, Papa, you must rest be-

tween acts and not make the effort to entertain anybody."

"I always promised your mother that you should have nothing to do with the theatre," Beau Bardsley said.

"And we will always do as Mama wished," Shimona replied, "but I know she would not have wanted me to leave you when you are as ill as you are now."

She looked at her father again and said in a low voice:

"Would you not be wiser to cancel the performance before it begins?"

There was every reason for her apprehension, for Beau Bardsley's handsome face was almost devoid of colour, his lips were bloodless, and he seemed to have difficulty in lifting his eye-lids.

"I have to go on," he said almost savagely. "For God's sake, Joe, give me some more brandy!"

The dresser snatched up the empty glass and hurried to the side of the room where there was a grog-table loaded with bottles and a large number of glasses.

Shimona knew only too well how much of her father's money was expended on entertaining the social personalities who fawned on him.

But he also played host to members of the cast whom he felt were in need of a stimulant and to whom he was always ready to extend an over-generous hand.

At least three quarters of Beau Bardsley's salary every week, his daughter reckoned, was given away to those who spun him a hard-luck story or who were genuinely in need.

There were many in the profession who blessed him for saving them from the gutter, from starvation, or from prison.

Because he had once played with them on the stage, or because they had a common interest, Beau Bardsley would feed, clothe, and pay the debts of any impoverished actor or actress who begged him for help.

Those who had suffered in consequence had of course been his own wife and daughter.

Despite all the years he had worked and commanded a high salary, he had no savings left. Every penny had been spent and the bulk of it on other actors.

Yet looking at him now Shimona knew that she would not have her father any different.

Even when he was ill, even when it was an effort for him to speak, he still had a magic quality about him.

It was his glamour which kept the audiences spellbound, and his deep resonant voice had a quality which seemed to draw the very hearts of those who listened.

The second glass of brandy brought a faint flush to Beau Bardsley's cheeks, and as the dresser deftly removed his coat and waist-coat he began with a hand which gradually became more steady to apply the grease-paint to his handsome countenance.

The son of a curate at Bath Abbey, Beau Bardsley, who had been christened Beaugrave, ran away when he was sixteen to go on the stage.

He had been obsessed by the theatre, which in Bath had reached the heights of distinction when it was honoured by being the first theatre outside London to be granted the title "Royal."

The actors and actresses who made their reputations there had no more eager and enthusiastic admirer than the clergyman's son.

After some years of playing small parts in the London theatres, including Drury Lane, Beau Bardsley had returned to his native town.

His father had been appointed to a living in another part of the country, and the theatre was filled with young and enthusiastic actors who were to become some of the greatest in the land.

John Henderson, who after five years at Bath went to London as David Garrick's natural successor, became one of England's leading actors.

He in his turn had been much struck by a young actress whom he had seen performing in Birmingham, and he recommended her to the Directors of the Bath Theatre, who engaged her.

As she had recently been dismissed by Garrick after a few unsuccessful months at Drury Lane, she was glad to have the chance to get before a fashionable audience, and this time she was no failure.

Sarah Siddons' debut in Bath was a triumph!

She was a phenomenal success, particularly in tragic roles.

Being a woman and an extremely intelligent one, she looked round to find actors who would enhance her own performance and intensify the glamour she exuded whenever she appeared behind the footlights.

It was therefore not surprising that she looked very favourably on the compellingly handsome Beau Bardsley.

Sarah Siddons was to be the greatest tragic actress of the English stage.

She was beautiful and she had an excellent figure, but these attributes were unimportant beside the power she could exert over an audience.

Beau Bardsley had been with her when in 1782 she had returned to the scene of her failure—the Theatre Royal, Drury Lane.

He had often told Shimona what happened.

"When Mrs. Siddons went on the stage at rehearsal she was in a state of panic," he related. "But gradually the play—*Isabelle, or The Fatal Marriage*—took hold of her and as it continued many of the company were in tears.

"She was so convincing in her death-bed scene," Beau Bardsley went on, "that her own eight-year-old son, Henry, who was playing the part of her son in the play, was actually deceived into believing that his mother had really died. He howled the place down until she finished the scene and comforted him."

"Tell me about the first night, Papa," Shimona would beg, even though she had heard the story over and over again.

Beau Bardsley would laugh.

"The audience were nearly drowned in tears," he replied, "and long before the final scene there was frenzied applause."

He smiled as he continued:

"I think we were all stunned by the ovation and Mrs. Siddons was too overcome to speak the Epilogue. She could only bow to a storm of cheers."

For the next one-and-twenty years Beau Bardsley had appeared in practically every important production in which Sarah Siddons played the lead.

But now she had gone, and although he could fill the theatre which had been rebuilt nine years earlier, he was at nearly fifty years of age almost too ill to carry on.

Shimona watched her father anxiously as, his make-up finished, he rose to his feet and went behind the brown linen curtain at the back of the room to change into his clothes for the First Act.

The new theatre had cost over £220,000 and had been designed by Holland, the architect of Carlton House. The dressing-rooms were certainly a great improvement on the discomfort, dirt, and darkness of the old ones.

Old Drury had been in a shocking state, having stood for 117 years since 1674.

But Shimona used to love hearing tales of what it had been like when her father first played there.

Then it had been easy to imagine Nell Gwynn selling oranges at sixpence apiece to the Gallants; Samuel Pepys, the diarist, ogling the women; and Charles II and his mistresses filling the Royal Box.

The audience would wander all over the stage and behind the scenes. There were "Fobs," who preened themselves, and "Vizards," who were ladies of the town disguised by black masks.

"Garrick drove the people from the stage," Beau Bardsley told his daughter, "but it was shove and push outside the Pit-entrance for hours before the doors opened."

"What happened then, Papa?" Shimona would ask.

"Men used their fists, the weakest were trampled underfoot, the pickpockets reaped a rich harvest!"

Beau Bardsley had performed in the last play at the old theatre, called *The Country Girl,* and he was in *Macbeth* with Mrs. Siddons when the new play-house was opened on April 21, 1794.

The house was packed on that occasion, but it had not proved a lucky building, and Richard Brinsley Sheridan was, everyone knew, deeply in debt.

Later Shimona had much admired the new Play-house from a box where her mother had taken her to watch her father perform although they were forbidden to enter the stage-door.

Certainly it was spacious and lofty.

There were four tiers and the boxes were on the lines of an Opera House, but Holland had thought more of appearance than of the convenience of the audience.

It was found that the Gallery was too high and so far away that its occupants had difficulty hearing the actors and the eight boxes on the stage itself and the eight on either side of the Pit were no use at all.

But the total capacity of the new Theatre Royal was 3,611 and in money £826.6s 0d.

It certainly had many modern requirements. There was even a fire-resistant curtain made of iron.

This, Beau Bardsley told Shimona, had been undoubtedly the star attraction of the opening nights and it aroused an already excited audience to a wild enthusiasm.

"Somebody struck it heavily with a large hammer," he told her, "to demonstrate its strength and solidarity."

"What happened then, Papa?" Shimona would ask, though she knew the end of the story perfectly well.

"When it was raised," her father replied, "the audience was thrilled by the sight of a cascade of water rushing down from tanks in the roof and roaring into a huge basin where it splashed and rumbled over artificial rocks."

"It must have been exciting!"

"It was!" her father agreed. "And when a man appeared in a boat and rowed about, the audience could scarcely contain itself!"

It was only when she grew older that Shimona

realised that what Sheridan had called his Grand National Theatre was unlucky from the very beginning, mostly owing to the disastrous condition of his finances.

From the highest to the lowest, payment of employees was spasmodic, and there were constant strikes.

Good actors were sacked because they demanded their overdue wages and their places were filled by inferior players.

On Saturday mornings the actors would besiege Sheridan's room.

"For God's sake, Mr. Sheridan," they would cry, "pay us our salaries. Let us have something this week!"

If he was there, he would turn on his charm and faithfully promise that he would pay what he owed them, then vanish by another door.

Only Shimona and her mother knew how much Beau Bardsley gave away to the poorest actors and staff, and how they suffered in consequence.

They had to forgo the little luxuries and even the good food to which they should have been entitled through the success that Beau Bardsley had achieved with the London audiences.

That he never worried was no answer to the problem, and yet, like those who watched him play his parts, they adored him, and his wife found it impossible even to grumble at the extravagant manner in which he helped others.

There was a sudden loud knock on the dressing-room door.

"Five minutes, Mr. Bardsley!" the call-boy shouted.

Then Shimona could hear him hurrying down the stone passage, hammering on every dressing-room door and repeating his parrot-cry.

Her father came from behind the curtain and she looked at him anxiously. But, as so often had happened, the atmosphere of the theatre was beginning to lift him out of himself.

Already he seemed to carry his shoulders straighter, his chin was higher, and his eyes were alight with

that irresistible magic which held the audience spellbound.

His costume became him, and his thinness, which
at times was pitiably obvious in his ordinary clothes,
made him, behind the footlights, look like the young
boy he was portraying.

He walked to the dressing-table, applied a little
more rouge to his face with the hare's foot, and
touched up the corners of his eyes.

"You look very handsome, Papa!"

It was something Shimona had said to him ever
since she was a small child and he smiled at her with
great tenderness before he replied:

"You will stay here while I am on the stage and
Joe is not to open the door to anybody."

"I'll see she's all right, Sir," Joe Hewitt promised.

"Two minutes, Mr. Bardsley!"

The call-boy's shrill voice accompanied by his
knock on the door seemed to lift the last remaining
remnants of Beau Bardsley's exhaustion from him.

He gave a last glance at himself in the mirror, then
turned towards the door.

"Good luck, Papa!"

He smiled at Shimona again, then he was gone and
she heard him speaking in his deep voice to several
people outside in the passage as they made their way
towards the stage.

She wished she could be at the front of the house
to see him performing one of his most memorable roles,
which invariably had evoked paeans of praise from the
critics.

One critic had written the previous week:

"I have run out of complimentary adjectives
where Beau Bardsley is concerned."

And the *Morning Chronicle* had said:

"The man ceases to be human as soon as he
appears, and he manages to transport himself
and his audience to the foothills of Olympus!"

Shimona rose from the red plush sofa on which she had been sitting and automatically began to tidy her father's dressing-table.

There was a miniature of her mother which he carried with him always: painted by Richard Cosway, it was, Shimona thought, an almost perfect likeness.

She looked so beautiful, so young and happy, and it seemed impossible to think that she was dead and they would never see her again.

Cosway had made her large eyes shine with the adoring light that had always been in them when she looked at her husband, and her fair hair had strange shadows in it which were faithfully portrayed against the soft blue background.

Holding the miniature in her hand, Shimona looked down at it with the pain in her heart that came whenever she thought of her mother.

How was it possible that she had died so suddenly and so quickly that they had not even realised she was ill until she was gone from them?

"We were always thinking of Papa," Shimona told herself now, "and we did not realise that Mama needed attention until it was too late!"

She felt an inescapable sense of loss stab her like a physical wound.

As she returned the miniature once again to its hook in the velvet case, she glanced at her own reflection in the mirror and saw how closely she resembled her mother.

She had the same pale shadowy fair hair, the same large eyes, the same oval forehead, the same softly curved lips.

There was also something of her father's looks in Shimona's face.

His Grecian profile seemed somehow to give him a spirituality which was seldom seen upon the stage, and it also made his daughter seem different from other young women of her age.

She was lovely, there was no doubt about that!

There was also something unique about her, which was one of the reasons why Beau Bardsley kept her away from the people who frequented his dressing-room at Drury Lane and whom, although he called them his friends, he never invited to his home.

Beau had always kept his family life strictly private from the moment he had caused one of the greatest scandals that Bath had ever known.

Because of it he had been determined not to expose his wife to the familiarity and the free and easy morals of the theatre world.

It was when he was playing some of his last parts at Bath with Mrs. Siddons before they both went to London that Beau Bardsley had noticed a girl in a stage-box.

It was not surprising that he became aware of her, for she was there day after day. She was usually accompanied in the afternoon by a maid or footman and in the evening by an elderly couple whom he learnt later were her father and mother.

There were plenty of people in Bath to tell him about Annabel Winslow.

Her beauty had taken the fashionable society which congregated in the Assembly-Rooms by storm.

She was fêted and sought after by the Dandies and Bucks of eligible age and she was adulated by the elderly noblemen who found her manners as charming as her appearance.

All Bath appeared to be delighted when Annabel's engagement to Lord Powell was announced, a gentleman whose wealth and distinction had already impressed itself upon the pleasure-seeking visitors to the famous Spa.

He had come to Bath because he was suffering with rheumatism in his legs, but after one look at Annabel his rheumatism was forgotten and he lost his heart!

Lord Powell's was undoubtedly the most important offer of marriage Annabel had received, and her father, Sir Harvey Winslow, lost no time in accepting on her behalf.

But no-one realised that if Lord Powell had lost his heart, Annabel had also lost hers.

Her parents had not concerned themselves with her passion for the theatre. After all, it was good for her education to listen to Shakespeare's plays, and Mrs. Siddons as Lady Macbeth and Desdemona was the talk of the Pump-Room.

Sir Harvey and Lady Winslow also thought her excellent in Garrick's version of *Hamlet* and they did not notice particularly the actor who played the name-part.

They were therefore stupefied with astonishment, as indeed was the rest of Bath, when Annabel ran away with Beau Bardsley.

When Mrs. Siddons left for London and Drury Lane, Annabel and Beau followed her.

Sir Harvey cut his daughter off with the proverbial shilling and returned to his Estates in Dorset, saying that he never wished to hear of her again.

Annabel was, however, supremely and utterly happy with the man she had chosen for her husband, and when Shimona was born in 1785 she thought it would be difficult for any woman to be more blessed than she had been.

From the time they married there was never another breath of scandal where Beau Bardsley was concerned.

It was to be expected that he would be pursued by women of every sort and kind; but while he was always courteous and pleasant, they found him elusive and impossible to meet outside the theatre.

As soon as a performance was over he went back to the little house in Chelsea where he lived with Annabel and Shimona and craved no other company but theirs.

Perhaps it was the puritanical streak in him which he had inherited from his clergyman father, or maybe a sense of guilt at his own shortcomings towards his parents, that made him ultra-strict with Shimona.

She had no idea that her life was different from that of other children or that she and her mother might have been living on a desert island for all the contact they had with other people.

From the moment Beau Bardsley left his home to the moment he returned there was always a feverish activity to get everything ready for him, to make his home-coming a perfect one.

From the time she was a tiny child Shimona was told, "You must not bother your father," "You must not upset him," "You must not worry him," and her whole object in life therefore was to make him happy.

The only amusement that was permitted outside the ordinary round of her life at home was when she and her mother went to the theatre to see her father in each new role.

It was then that he seemed to her to be a very different person from the man who held her on his knee to kiss and fondle her.

On the stage her father became a Knight like those of whom she read in story-books.

There was something inspiring and spiritual about him too, which made him seem almost like the angels in which she had believed ever since her mother had taught her to say her prayers.

If the audiences worshipped Beau Bardsley for his looks and the magical hours of pleasure he gave them, his daughter worshipped him because to her he was everything that was fine and noble personified in one man.

Beau Bardsley had, despite his father's poverty, been well educated.

He had been accepted in private schools at reduced rates because his father was a clergyman and the parts he played also gave him a command of the English language and a knowledge of history which he imparted to his daughter.

Although she never went to school and never competed with other children, Shimona was far better educated than was considered necessary for the average girl at that time.

In fact, through her father's tuition she received to all intents and purposes a boy's education, while her mother imparted the accomplishments which were considered obligatory for a well-bred young woman.

When her mother died Shimona experienced a loneliness that she had never encountered before.

Now there were long days at home when there was nothing to do but talk to her old Nurse and await her father's return.

Because she was lonely and because time often hung heavy on her hands she started to read the newspapers and enjoy all the anecdotes and gossip that her father brought home in the evenings.

Whereas before her death Beau Bardsley had talked with his wife about the problems and quarrels of the theatre and about those who visited his dressing-room with their scandal and gossip, he now talked to Shimona.

She had always been excluded in the past from anything that appertained to the outside world, but now because his wife was no longer beside him Beau allowed Shimona to take her place.

For almost the first time, Shimona, at eighteen, began to realise that she was missing something.

She heard about Balls, Assemblies, Receptions, great parties at Carlton House, and dinner at Almack's Club, where one had to receive a voucher from one of the distinguished hostesses before being admitted.

"Will I ever be able to go to a Ball, Papa?" she asked Beau one evening.

He had returned from the theatre to tell Shimona how he had refused an invitation to a party at the Duke of Richmond's at which the Prince of Wales was to be present.

Beau Bardsley looked at his daughter as if he saw her for the first time.

She was very lovely in a muslin gown with its high waist outlining the soft curves of her breasts, and her skin was very white against the red velvet chair on which she was sitting.

In fact she looked so lovely that he drew in his breath as he remembered that his wife, Annabel, had looked almost exactly the same when they had first met.

"A Ball, my dearest?" he repeated, his thoughts elsewhere.

"Yes, Papa. Have you forgotten that I am eighteen? Mama told me about the Ball that was given for her when she made her début, and I would so love to go to one myself."

Beau Bardsley stared at her for a long time, then he said:

"It is impossible!"

"Why?" Shimona enquired.

He rose to his feet to walk across the room as if he was finding words in which to answer her and finally he said:

"You might as well face the truth. The *Beau Monde* invited me to their houses because I am a celebrity—a celebrity but merely an actor. It amuses them to condescend to those who have reached the top of their profession."

His voice sharpened as he went on:

"But while they will accept me, their wives and daughters would not accept my wife and daughter."

"Why not, Papa?"

"Because an actor can never be the social equal of those of noble birth. Because I am what I have made myself—you must suffer."

Shimona gazed at him wide-eyed before she said hesitatingly:

"Although you are an actor, you are a . . . gentleman, Papa. Your father was a Canon before he died . . . Mama told me so."

"My father was ashamed of me," Beau Bardsley replied. "He planned that I should enter the Church. He envisaged me inspiring a congregation with my oratory from the pulpit."

He smiled a little wryly.

"I doubt if my congregation would ever have filled Drury Lane."

"And the Winslows were a County family and much respected in Dorset," Shimona persisted.

"And how often have you been asked to stay

with your grandfather and grandmother?" Beau Bardsley asked.

There was a long silence.

"I think . . . I understand."

"If I was meant to be punished for running away with your mother and being given the greatest happiness any man could ever know on earth, it is now," Beau Bardsley said, "because, my dearest, I cannot give you all the things I would wish to."

Shimona had run into his arms.

"You are not to think about it, Papa. I am happy, terribly happy, just to be with you. Do you think I worry about Balls when I can watch you on the stage and we can be together when you come home?"

Beau Bardsley had not replied. He merely bent his head and kissed his daughter on the cheek.

Then he said almost beneath his breath:

"The Bible is right. The sins of the fathers *are* visited upon the children."

Shimona had heard the pain in her father's voice, and never again had she mentioned the fashionable world or the irrepressible longing she felt at times to be part of it. But she listened even more intently to her father's stories.

Every evening when he returned home, while he ate his supper she would ask who had visited him in his dressing-room and who was in the principal boxes in the theatre.

She also coaxed him into telling her stories about the social personalities of the *Beau Monde*.

It was not that she wished to listen to scandal; it was just that she was curious about the people who lived in the world outside the little house in Chelsea, who were very much less real to her than the characters of Shakespeare or those whom she loved in Sheridan's *School for Scandal*.

Sir Peter Teazle, Sir Benjamin Backbite, and Sir Harry Bumper all meant much more in her life than the Prince of Wales and the Bucks and Dandies who accompanied him when he occupied the Royal Box at Drury Lane.

When she visited the theatre Shimona would look round her and try to identify some of the people about whom her father talked.

Now as she waited in the dressing-room she heard the applause beginning to roar out like distant thunder, and rising to her feet she opened the door so that it came to her in great waves of sound.

She knew that once again her father's magic had infected the audience to the point where they would be rising in their seats, clapping and cheering him as he took bow after bow.

She stood in the open doorway and looked down the long passage which was dimly lit by candles in wooden sconces.

It was then that Shimona remembered that the other actors also would be returning to their dressing-rooms and quickly she shut the door.

Her father came in followed by Joe, who had been waiting for him in the wings. Now his cheeks were flushed and there was a light in his eyes which was always there after a particularly successful performance.

"They loved you, Papa!"

"It went well," Beau Bardsley answered.

He turned towards his dressing-table and as he did so he was suddenly seized by a fit of coughing.

It was as if it had been held back for so long that now it was a paroxysm that racked his whole frame so that he coughed and coughed until it seemed that the very sound of it must tear him to pieces.

Joe and Shimona helped him to the chair, and when finally the spasm ceased the sweat was pouring down Beau Bardsley's forehead and his eyes were closed.

He was shaking and once again it was a glass of brandy and water that revived him.

This time Shimona knew that Joe had made it even stronger than it had been before.

It was an effort to get her father changed in time and an almost superhuman effort, she was well aware, for him to obey the call-boy's voice as he shouted imperiously:

"One minute, Mr. Bardsley!"

There was a note of rebuke because the leading actor was not already in the wings.

Joe went with his master to the stage, then came back.

"He's bad, Miss Shimona!" he said abruptly as he came into the dressing-room.

"I know, Joe, but he will not rest. I begged him not to come today."

"He'll kill himself, Miss Shimona. You mark my words!"

Shimona stifled a little cry which came to her lips.

"The Doctor said the same . . . thing, but he will not . . . listen and . . . and he has to work."

"I understands, Miss."

"You have been with him for so many years, Joe. You know as well as I do that he has never saved a penny."

"I knows, Miss, and on Saturday morning they'll be round him like hawks. I often thinks as how he never touches his wages himself. So many other fingers are a-digging at it."

"If he can keep going a little . . . longer he will get a . . . benefit," Shimona said.

"He's due for one, Lord knows!" Joe said. "But the theatre ain't doing well except when the master's playing, an' I has a feeling the management thinks that if he gets a benefit he might go off on a holiday."

"That is exactly when he ought to do," Shimona replied. "The Doctor said only yesterday that he should go to a warmer climate for the winter. It will be November soon and he will never stand the fogs and the cold winds."

They looked at each other anxiously and then, as if he could not bring himself to speak of it any more, Joe said:

"I'm taking a glass of brandy to the stage. If he has another coughing fit it's the only thing that'll enable him to carry on."

Shimona did not answer. She only sat down on the sofa again.

The future seemed bleak. She wondered what her mother would have done.

She looked across the small dressing-room at the miniature standing on the dressing-table.

"Oh, Mama," she whispered, "help us. How can Papa go on like this? Joe says he will kill himself and then what will happen to me? Please, Mama, please help us! You must know the trouble we are in."

She felt the tears come into her eyes as she spoke.

Then because she was afraid that her father might notice if she cried, she quickly wiped them away.

Shimona could never bear to remember how distraught he had been when her mother died. At times she thought he would go insane, and because she had to give him her strength she had never let herself cry in front of him.

Sometimes she thought it was all that had sustained him, all that had prevented him from collapsing completely.

There was another long wait. Then at last she heard the applause break out and knew that the play had ended.

"I must get Papa home as quickly as possible," she told herself. "Joe can call us a carriage which will be waiting at the door and Nanna will have supper ready. Then he must go straight to bed."

She wondered if it would be wiser for him not to change but to go home as he was.

Her father was always very fastidious about his appearance, but there would be nobody to see him and his long grey cloak would conceal the velvet costume he wore as Hamlet.

"I am sure that would be wise," Shimona decided.

Now the noise in the distance was gradually subsiding and she heard the voices of the actors outside in the passage. Then she heard her father say:

"If you will just wait a moment, Your Grace, I will look and see if the dressing-room is tidy."

"My dear Bardsley, I have been in enough dressing-rooms not to worry whether they are tidy or not," came the reply.

Shimona knew immediately that her father was saying this to warn her that he had a visitor, and rising she quickly slipped behind the curtain as the door opened.

"As I might have expected," she heard an amused voice remark, "your dressing-room is a model of neatness, and certainly there are no suspicious petticoats about!"

"No, Your Grace."

Beau Bardsley spoke abruptly as if he resented the insinuation.

"I know you want to get home, Bardsley," his visitor went on. "I am well aware how you hate to hang about after the performance is over, but I have to see you—I need your help."

Beau Bardsley gave a light laugh.

"My help? How can I possibly be of help to the Duke of Ravenstone?"

Shimona, listening, knew that her father was in his own fashion informing her who was present, and at the same time warning her that she must on no account reveal her presence.

She had heard him speak of the Duke of Ravenstone, and everything he had said about him came to her mind as she listened intently.

"Will you have a drink, Your Grace?"

"No, thank you."

Shimona realised without being able to see him that the Duke had seated himself on the sofa she had just vacated.

"I will come straight to the point," he said. "I need an actress. . . ."

"Then you have come to the wrong man, Your Grace," Beau Bardsley interrupted sharply. "As you are well aware, I never effect introductions to the members of the cast in this or in any other theatre."

The Duke laughed.

"My dear Bardsley, you are barking up the wrong tree! If I wanted to meet an actress for my own needs I would have no difficulty in meeting her, and I certainly would not need you to introduce me!"

"Then how can I help you?" Beau Bardsley asked in a different tone.

"It is a long story, but I will be brief," the Duke replied. "My sister married a Scotsman by name of McCraig. He is now dead, but my nephew Alister Mc-Craig is very much alive and was married over a year ago to Kitty Varden. You remember Kitty?"

"Good Lord, of course I do!" Beau Bardsley exclaimed. "But I had no idea that McCraig was your nephew!"

"I do not trouble myself with relatives as a rule," the Duke continued. "In fact they bore me to distraction, but I knew Kitty when she was on the boards. Who did not?"

He paused as if waiting for confirmation of this and automatically Beau Bardsley answered:

"As Your Grace says—who did not?"

"Surprisingly, she has made my nephew very happy, but Kitty is still Kitty! Though she may no longer be acting, she still looks very much the same as she did when she sang those bawdy songs which nearly took the roof off!"

"I remember them," Beau remarked drily.

"Then you can imagine that with her red hair and her voluptuous bosom, which seems to have grown even more ample in the last two years, she is hardly likely to impress her husband's Great-Uncle—The Mc-Craig of McCraig!"

"I seem to have heard of him," Beau Bardsley remarked.

"Some people call him the uncrowned King of Scotland, which is certainly true where his own Clan are concerned, and he is, incidentally, an extremely rich man."

Shimona heard her father move restlessly, as if he was longing to reach the end of the story.

"I am sorry to bore you with this," the Duke remarked, "but the position quite simply is that for years my sister has been trying to make The McCraig take an interest in Alister, but he can leave his own money where he wishes."

Shimona thought that by this time her father would be as interested as she was.

"Go on," she heard him say.

"The McCraig, out of the blue, has notified his intention of coming to London. He wishes to see the Prime Minister on Scottish Affairs and he has informed my nephew Alister that he would like to meet his wife."

The Duke paused for a moment before he went on:

"There is no doubt that if he approves of the marriage, he will, as my sister has been trying to persuade him to do, make Alister his heir."

There was silence before Beau Bardsley said:

"Speaking frankly, Your Grace, it is hardly likely he will approve of Kitty."

"That is very obvious, not only to you and me, but also to Alister."

Again there was a pause before the Duke continued:

"That is why you are the only person who can help me, Bardsley."

"How can I do that?"

"You can find me an actress who will play the part of my nephew's wife for two days. That is all I require. Just two days for a woman to act the part of a lady sufficiently well to convince a dour old Scot that she is a suitable wife for his heir."

"Are you serious?" Beau Bardsley asked.

"Completely!" the Duke answered. "I have thought hard about this, and it is to my mind the only possible way that Alister can receive a large sum of money now and inherit something like a million when The McCraig dies!"

"As much as that?"

"It might be more!"

"Do you really think he can be deceived by someone acting a part?"

"Good God, why not?" the Duke exclaimed. "You fellows create an illusion and make people believe anything you want them to. Half the women present in the audience tonight were crying when you died."

"It is different behind the footlights," Beau Bardsley murmured.

"An actor's job is to present an illusion and make it seem real," the Duke remarked. "Whatever you say or do, the audience believes it to be the truth. I am asking for a woman to make a man of eighty believe that she is a decent, respectable person. It should not be very hard."

"I find it almost impossible to think of anyone who could do that," Beau Bardsley said.

"I admit it might not be easy to find someone who looks and sounds right," the Duke conceded after a moment. "But you are a gentleman, Bardsley, and that is why I came to you. I do not want the dross showing through the gold too quickly."

Beau Bardsley was silent for some seconds before he said:

"For the moment I cannot think of a single soul who could play such a part. There is Judith Page, who rather specialises in Ladies of Quality, but she is too old. There is Sylvia Verity."

"Good God, not her!" the Duke ejaculated. "One drink and the polish comes off that refined accent!"

"I know," Beau Bardsley conceded.

"There must be someone—perhaps someone new in the theatre," the Duke persisted. "She does not have to do much, beyond keeping quiet, and I will teach her the few lines that are necessary."

Beau Bardsley must have looked at him, for he said quickly:

"Nothing like that, Bardsley, I promise! This is strictly business, and, if the girl is pure, then she will leave my house as pure as she came—that I promise you!"

"*Your* house?" Beau Bardsley questioned.

"My nephew is at present staying with me at Ravenstone House in Berkeley Square. I have invited The McCraig to be my guest for the two days he is in London. I will take every care to see that your protégée is not alone with him at any time. Either Alister or myself will be there to bridge any uncomfortable moment and to answer any difficult questions."

Beau Bardsley did not speak and the Duke went on:

"Perhaps I should have mentioned already that I consider a proper fee for this piece of exceptional acting would be five hundred guineas!"

He laughed.

"You look surprised, Bardsley."

"It is a lot of money, Your Grace!"

"I am prepared to pay that and any more that is required to ensure that my nephew inherits his Great-Uncle's money. As I have already told you, it is worth taking trouble for a million!"

"I suppose it might be possible to find someone suitable," Beau Bardsley conceded. "You know as well as I do, Your Grace, there are thousands who would jump at the chance of earning that sort of money! But they might let you down—it is not worth the risk!"

"I knew you would be the only person who would understand," the Duke said. "That is why I have forced myself on you when you made it obvious that you did not wish to talk to me."

"I must apologise if I seemed impolite."

"Not at all! We all know you return to your house in Chelsea to be with your family, who must not be contaminated by people like myself."

The Duke spoke with laughter in his voice and he went on:

"Your obsession for privacy may cause resentment in some quarters, Bardsley, but as far as I am concerned, I admire you for it!"

"I thank Your Grace."

Shimona heard the Duke rise to his feet.

"If you fail me, Bardsley," he said, "then I swear I will put you at the top of my long list of enemies!"

"I only wish you would ask the assistance of somebody else," Beau Bardsley said.

"You know the answer to that," the Duke replied. "There is no-one else—no-one else who would understand what the hell I am talking about! I want a *Lady,*

Bardsley, and I do not believe there is any other actor in this theatre who would know one if he met one."

"You are very scathing, Your Grace."

"God knows, I do not intend to be. I suppose I have had more fun in the theatres of London than any other man alive," the Duke remarked. "Do you remember Perdita? And Rosa Lenin? And that attractive little creature who screamed the place down when I tried to be rid of her? What was her name?"

"Betty Wilson!"

"Yes, of course! Betty Wilson! She even hired men to break the windows of Ravenstone House. I cannot see any of them acting the part, can you? No, Bardsley, you and I know exactly what is required, and, as I said before, only you are capable of finding her."

"I think it will prove impossible!" Beau Bardsley said slowly.

"Then I will tell you what I will do," the Duke said. "I will give the lady—and she had better look like one—five hundred guineas, and there will be another five hundred guineas for you to squander on the rag, tag, and bobtail who come to you with stories of their old mothers dying in cold garrets! One thousand guineas, Bardsley! That should make it worth your while."

There was no answer, then the Duke added:

"Send your choice to me at Ravenstone House an hour before noon tomorrow. That should give my nephew and me time to instruct her in the fundamentals of the situation before the old boy arrives for luncheon."

The Duke opened the door.

"One thousand guineas, my dear man! It is worth thinking about!"

Chapter Two

Beau Bardsley sank back against the cushions of the hired carriage and shut his eyes.

His cloak was wrapped over the black velvet suit which he had worn in the last act of the play, but he had removed the make-up from his face and in the flickering lights from the linkmen's lanterns Shimona could see how pale he was.

They drove for some way in silence before she said tentatively:

"Will you be . . . able to do what the Duke . . . asked?"

"I should imagine it would be quite impossible to find the sort of woman he requires at such short notice."

Her father's voice did not sound too exhausted, and after a moment Shimona said:

"We need five hundred guineas, Papa."

"I know that, but playing a part off the stage is very different from playing one on it."

"Why?"

"Because actors speak the lines they are given, and most of the women in the profession are uneducated and of a doubtful character."

There was silence, and then as if he knew what his daughter was thinking Beau Bardsley said quickly:

"Not Sarah Siddons: she indeed was different. But it would be much easier to find an actor to look and behave like a gentleman than an actress to play a lady."

Again there was silence before Shimona said in a very small voice:

"We need five hundred guineas, Papa, desperately! I . . . suppose I could not . . . play the . . . part for . . . you?"

Beau Bardsley was suddenly rigid and it seemed as if he was stunned into silence. Then he said:

"Are you crazy? Do you think for one moment that I would allow you to do such a thing or to go to the house of that man?"

"I have heard you . . . speak of the Duke, Papa."

"Then you know how disreputable he is and how much I despise him."

"But why, Papa? What has he done?"

"He stands for everything that is lecherous and debauched. Do you know what they call him behind his back?"

"No, Papa. How should I?"

"He is known as 'His Disgrace,' and it is an apt designation."

"But, Papa, what does he do?"

"I would not soil your ears with repeating the scandals in which he has been involved, or the menace he is to women, not only in his own world but also in the theatre and the night-haunts of London."

"You mean that he . . . pursues women?"

"And they pursue him," Beau Bardsley answered. "He has more charm in his little finger than most men have in their whole body, and he uses it entirely to his own ends."

Her father spoke so violently that Shimona looked at him apprehensively in case it should bring on another fit of coughing.

"I have seen too many of the hearts that Ravenstone has broken," he went on, "the lives he has disrupted and ruined, the chaos he has caused in one way or another! If you want the truth, I loathe him!"

"You were polite to him, Papa."

"How could I be anything else?" Beau Bardsley asked. "A nobleman in his position could do me irreparable harm if I chose to make an enemy of him."

"How could he do that?" Shimona asked.

"There is no point in discussing it. I shall have to

try to do as he wishes. I only hope to God I can think
of some young woman who would be suitable."

There was silence, until Beau Bardsley said almost savagely:

"You would think he could find someone himself.
He knows enough women, but of course they are not
the sort who would deceive anyone."

Shimona said no more, but as they journeyed on
she began to pray that her father would find the
woman the Duke wanted and earn the five hundred
guineas.

With that much money he could go abroad as
the Doctor wished.

In the sunshine of Italy she was sure that his
cough would go, and he would put on weight and be
strong again as he had been when she was a child.

Always then he had seemed full of exciting and
irrepressible vitality that made the tempo rise the
moment he entered a room.

"Papa is back, Mama!"

She could hear her voice screaming with excitement as she ran helter-skelter down the stairs to open
the front door before her father could raise his hand to
the knocker.

"Papa! Papa!"

Her arms would go round his neck and he would
lift her off her feet, swinging her round until she was
giddy or tickling her until she laughed hysterically.

Then he had been very unlike the pale-faced man
who now crept back to Chelsea every night, often too
tired to eat the delicious suppers which Nanna cooked
for him.

"He must rest! He must get away!" Shimona told
herself.

Once again she was praying to her mother for
help, feeling that wherever she was in the Heaven in
which she so fervently believed she would somehow
contrive to be near the man she had loved with all her
heart and soul.

"You must help us, Mama," Shimona said beneath
her breath. "Papa will die if he goes on like this!"

Now the carriage had reached Sloane Square and was proceeding down King's Road.

"As soon as Papa has had something to eat," Shimona told herself, "he must go to bed. If he means to find the actress that the Duke requires, he will have to be up early to go in search of her."

The horses came to a standstill and Shimona put her hand on her father's arm.

"We are home, Papa!"

"Home . . . ?"

It seemed for a moment as if Beau Bardsley was dazed and uncertain of what he was saying. Then with an effort he followed Shimona from the carriage, bending his head to do so.

It might have been that or the wind whistling round the corner which started him coughing.

He stood on the pavement doubled up with the paroxysm which shook him once again.

Nanna, who had been waiting for them, opened the door, and while he was still coughing they helped Beau Bardsley up the steps and into the small hall.

The rasping sound he was making seemed to echo round the walls.

"Let's get the Master upstairs," Nanna said to Shimona. "We'll try to persuade him to go straight to bed, but if he comes down again he'll wish to change."

Shimona put her arm round her father's waist, but the cabman who had followed them into the house intervened.

"'Ere, I'll 'elp 'is Nibs," he said. "An' proud to do it! Me an' the missus have waited many an hour to see 'im on the stage."

Beau Bardsley was not coughing so violently now but he was swaying with exhaustion and it seemed as if he might have fallen to the floor had not Nanna been holding him.

The cabman moved to his other side and he and Nanna almost literally carried him up the stairs to the front room.

It was Shimona's mother who had insisted that the

best room in the house, which should have been her
Drawing-Room, should be a bed-room.

"Papa is home so little," she had said to Shimona,
"and we never entertain. It will be much better to
make the bed-room into a place where he can not only
rest but study."

The front room, therefore, with its three long
windows opening onto the tree-lined Square outside,
was furnished with all the treasures which Shimona's
mother had collected over the years.

There was also a sofa and some chairs, so that it
was like a Sitting-Room, and usually Beau would lie in
bed while his wife sat beside the fire and sewed.

Shimona, when she was a child, would sit cross-
legged beside him, reading him extracts from her
fairy-stories.

Although she had not realised it, this had been a
lesson in elocution, because her father would check her
if she did not pronounce every word accurately with
the intonation and timing for which he himself was
famous.

Now when they reached the landing Shimona ran
ahead to take the cover from the bed so that the cabman and Nanna could lift Beau Bardsley onto the
top of the blankets and lay him back gently against
the pillows.

"Thank you," Shimona said to the man as he
turned towards the door. "How much do we owe
you?"

"Oi'll take nothin' from th' Guv'nor," the cabby
answered. "It's payment enough, as ye might say, for
the pleasure 'e's given me."

"Oh, thank you!" Shimona exclaimed.

It always touched her when people spoke in such
a way about her father.

"Nah ye look after 'im," the cabman admonished
as he started down the stairs. "Oi don' loik the looks
of 'im, an' that's a fact! Ye'd best get the Doctor right
away or The Lane'll lose the greatest actor it's ever 'ad."

"I will do that and thank you," Shimona said as she
shut the front door behind him.

She ran up the stairs to find Nanna outside the bed-room looking apprehensively at the handkerchief which she held in her hand.

"What ... is it?" Shimona asked in a whisper.

"We have to call the Doctor," Nanna said. "He's coughing blood, and it's not right—it's not right at all!"

"I will go!"

"At this time of night?" Nanna asked. "You'll do nothing of the sort. You'll find his warm milk ready on the stove. Persuade him to drink it and I'll get back as quickly as I can."

"Wait a moment!" Shimona cried. "I will ask the cabman to go for Dr. Lesley."

She ran down the stairs and managed to stop the hackney-carriage just as it was driving off.

The cabman heard Shimona calling him from the steps and pulled in his horse immediately.

"Wot is it, Missy?"

"Would you be kind enough to ask the Doctor to come to my father?" Shimona asked. "You are right. He is very ill. Very ill indeed!"

"Oi'll fetch 'im for yer. Where's 'e live, Miss?"

"Not far away in Eaton Square," Shimona answered. "At number eighty-two, and his name is Dr. Lesley."

"Leave it to me!" the cabman said, and whipping up his horse set off at a pace which told Shimona that he realised how urgent the matter was.

It was with great difficulty that she and Nanna managed to get her father undressed and into bed by the time Dr. Lesley arrived.

He was a blunt, good-natured man who had a great reputation amongst the top professionals of the theatrical world. He had in fact met Beau Bardsley through Richard Brinsley Sheridan, whom he had attended for many years.

He was, Shimona knew, not only her father's Doctor, but also a friend and an admirer of his talent, and her mother had trusted him implicitly.

He had been a tower of strength when Mrs. Bardsley had died, and Shimona often thought that if

it had not been for Dr. Lesley her father would have
had a nervous breakdown and made no effort to con-
tinue with his acting career.

When Shimona met him in the hall, Dr. Lesley
smiled at her, which proclaimed his affection more
effectively than any words.

"Oh, Dr. Lesley, I knew you would come when
you got my message!" Shimona said breathlessly.

"It was fortunate that I was still at home," he
replied. "I was just about to leave to visit an elderly
Countess, but she can wait! How bad is your father?"

"Very bad! He got through the performance tonight but it was only with the help of brandy, and
now he seems to have collapsed. Nanna says he is
coughing . . . blood!"

The Doctor's lips tightened.

"It is what I expected," he said. "I told you long
ago that he should rest and that you must get him
away to a warmer climate. These cold winds are mur-
der to a man in his condition."

"I know," Shimona said miserably.

"I suppose there is no money in the kitty as usual?" Dr. Lesley remarked as he started to climb the
stairs.

Shimona did not bother to answer.

Dr. Lesley knew as well as she did how every
penny her father earned was given away with a generous hand.

The Doctor went into the bed-room, telling Shimona to wait.

She went downstairs to the small Sitting-Room at
the back of the house which she and her mother had
used when they were alone.

It always seemed to her to be redolent with her
mother's presence.

It was here she had done her lessons; it was here
they had sat and talked during the long afternoons
and evenings when her father was at the theatre.

It was in this room that her mother had imparted
to her daughter her own simple philosophy of life,
which Shimona had tried to make her own.

And everywhere there were portraits and mementoes of her father.

The picture over the mantelpiece had been painted just before he had run away from Bath with the beautiful Annabel Winslow.

There was a miniature of him by Richard Cosway executed at the same time as he had commissioned the miniature of his wife.

There were sketches of him in his greatest roles, and caricatures which had been drawn by some of the most famous cartoonists in the land.

There were theatre posters and special tributes which Beau had received from time to time from the towns where he had played or from the company with whom he had acted.

'Mama loved him so much,' Shimona thought to herself. 'Why can she not help him now?'

Then insidiously, almost as if someone were saying it, the thought came to her of the thousand guineas which could be earned so easily if only her father would allow her to do so.

Then she remembered the anger in his voice when she suggested it and knew it would be impossible for her to persuade him.

The door opened and Dr. Lesley came in.

Shimona did not speak. She only looked at him, and knew what he was going to say before his lips moved.

"Your father is very ill, my dear," he said after a moment.

"Do you mean . . . that he is going to . . . die?" Shimona asked in a voice he could hardly hear.

"Yes, unless we do something positive to prevent it," Dr. Lesley replied.

"What can we do?"

"First, there is no question of his going on stage tomorrow or for a long time ahead," the Doctor said. "Secondly, we have to get him out of London and if possible to a warm climate."

He put his hand on Shimona's shoulder as he went on:

"I know the circumstances you are in, my dear, and I think the only thing I can do is to try to raise the money from your father's friends and admirers."

He gave a sigh.

"I have a feeling it is likely to be much easier for your father to give than to receive."

"That is true," Shimona answered. "And he would hate feeling that he was asking for charity."

"There is no alternative," Dr. Lesley said, "and I promise you, Shimona, I am not speaking lightly when I say that time is important. We have to get him away!"

Shimona clasped her hands together. Then she said:

"I have a chance, Doctor . . . of . . . earning one thousand guineas. But could you keep Papa from being . . . aware of what I am . . . doing?"

She saw an expression in the Doctor's face which made her say quickly:

"It is nothing really wrong; but Papa, as you know, does not like me to do anything outside the house."

"Will you tell me what it is?" Dr. Lesley asked.

Shimona hesitated.

"It is a . . . secret, and it is not . . . mine. All I can say is that . . . someone asked Papa tonight to find a . . . woman who would act a . . . certain part for two days."

"And for that they are prepared to pay one thousand guineas?" Dr. Lesley asked, and she heard the suspicion in his voice.

"It is a difficult part," she explained, "and in fact could only be played by someone who is . . . well born."

"You are sure it will not involve you in anything—unsavoury?"

The Doctor hesitated before the last word.

"I promise you I will not be involved in anything which you or even Mama would think wrong or damaging to me personally."

She looked up at the Doctor pleadingly.

"It is only Papa who is prejudiced against my meeting anyone outside this house."

"Your father is almost fanatical on the subject."

"That is why he must not know what I am doing," Shimona said. "But I shall be able to earn one thousand guineas, with which I can take him abroad, and he can rest until he is really well again."

"It certainly seems a solution to the problem," Dr. Lesley said slowly. "At the same time, I wish you could be a little more explicit."

Shimona did not answer.

She had the feeling that if she told the Doctor that the Duke was involved, he would, like her father, refuse to allow her to go to Ravenstone House.

The Duke had promised that he himself would not interfere with anyone who was willing to play the part.

There had been, Shimona thought, an unmistakable note of sincerity in his voice when he had said:

"This is strictly business, and if the girl is pure she will leave my house as pure as she came—that I promise!"

"It will be all right, I know it will be all right," she said to Dr. Lesley. "But in no circumstances must you let Papa know about it."

The Doctor stood staring into the fire for a few minutes before he said:

"God knows if I am doing the right thing, but it is actually a case of saving your father's life."

"Then why should you . . . hesitate?"

He turned his head to look at her.

"I am very fond of you, my child. I have known you since you were a little girl and I have watched you grow up into a very beautiful young woman. I would never forgive myself if you were harmed in any way."

"I am sure I will not be," Shimona said quickly.

"You know nothing of the world," Dr. Lesley said, "and to a young woman it can be a very dangerous place."

"If what I am doing at any time seems . . . dangerous," Shimona answered, "then I promise you I will come back straight away."

"You promise me that?"

"I promise!"

The Doctor parted his lips as if to say something else, then he changed his mind.

"Very well!" he said abruptly. "I will trust your judgement and I will keep your father from knowing what is happening."

"How will you do that?" Shimona enquired.

"He will sleep tonight after what I have given him to prevent him from coughing," the Doctor replied. "I will call early tomorrow morning and see that he sleeps through tomorrow and the following day."

Shimona put out her hands.

"Thank you, Doctor. I knew that you would not fail us. Mama always said you were the kindest man she had ever met."

"And because I admired your mother more than any other woman I have ever known I feel responsible for you," the Doctor said, "so for God's sake, my dear, take care of yourself!"

"I am quite confident I can do so," Shimona replied.

The Doctor turned towards the door.

"I shall be wondering all night whether it would have been better to collect the money from among your father's friends."

"I should be surprised if you managed to raise anything like one thousand guineas!"

"And if I am honest, so should I!" the Doctor replied.

He picked up his cloak, which he had left in the hall, set his hat on his head, and opened the front door.

Outside his smart Brougham was waiting, and as soon as he stepped into it the coachman set off in the direction of the West End.

Slowly Shimona went upstairs.

She went into the bed-room where Nanna had

blown out the candles, but by the light of the fire she could see that her father was asleep.

He looked more relaxed and therefore younger than when they had left the theatre.

He was breathing evenly, and it was difficult to realise that unless she could do something about it he was under sentence of death.

"I must save Papa . . . I must!" Shimona told herself.

Then she thought that the fact that she could earn one thousand guineas had been a direct answer to a prayer.

Perhaps her mother knew all about it and through some Divine Power they could not understand had sent them this life-line.

"If she can do that," Shimona asked, "why should there be any reason for me to be afraid?"

Her mother would protect her even in Ravenstone House.

* * *

The Duke walked into the Library and found his nephew, Alister McCraig, standing in front of the fire and reading the *Morning Post*.

"Good-morning, Uncle Yvell," he said as the Duke entered.

"Good-morning, Alister. I hope I have solved your troubles for you."

Alister McCraig put down the newspaper and looked eagerly at the Duke.

He was a nice-looking young man of twenty-five, with a pleasant but rather stupid face and fair hair with a touch of red in it.

It would have been difficult to mistake him for anything but a soldier: he had in fact served in a Regiment of the Brigade of Guards until, when he married an actress, he had been forced to resign his Commission.

"You have found someone to act the part?" Alister McCraig asked.

"Not yet, but Bardsley will find someone for me. I made sure of that!"

"How did you make sure of it?"

"I offered him so much money that it would be almost impossible for him to refuse to do as I wish," the Duke answered.

"That was very kind of you, Uncle Yvell. But you know I could never pay you back unless Great-Uncle Hector coughs up, as we hope he will."

"I am not asking you to pay me back," the Duke answered. "I am hoping you will get your fortune and then I need never bother about you again!"

"You have been damned kind over this, Uncle Yvell, and I shall never forget it," Alister McCraig said. "You are the only member of the family who has spoken to me since I married Kitty."

"You must admit it came as something of a shock to the majority of them," the Duke said in an amused voice. "It would have done the sanctimonious old hypocrites a lot of good, were it not that it was likely to leave you a pauper the rest of your life!"

"I am well aware of that!" Alister McCraig said.

There was a faint flush on his cheeks, and the Duke thought it was understandable how Kitty with her shrewd little brain and an eye for the main chance had thought it worthwhile to leave the stage for a husband who would be chivalrous and considerate to her for the rest of her life.

There was no doubt that Kitty had caught and enslaved Alister deliberately and, the Duke thought, with the sole object of becoming respectable.

She had enjoyed a long line of distinguished lovers before Alister had become infatuated with her.

Yet no-one had suspected for one moment that beneath her exuberant and rather disreputable career she had always longed for the security of a wedding-ring.

'Well, she has achieved her ambition,' the Duke thought, 'and there is nothing anyone can do about it.'

At the same time, he was determined if possible to save Alister from the worst consequences of his extremely ill-advised marriage.

A rich man would always be forgiven an offence

for which a poor one would be ostracised indefinitely.

"I suppose your mother has never seen Kitty?" the Duke asked.

"As you know, for some years she has not been well enough to travel South from Northumberland, and I have made innumerable excuses not to take Kitty to see her."

"Quite right!" the Duke approved. "There is no point in upsetting her."

"None at all," Alister McCraig agreed, "but I had no idea that she was still trying to get Great-Uncle Hector interested in me."

"I wonder how she has managed to do it," the Duke said reflectively.

He seated himself in a wing-back chair by the fireside and was looking at his nephew with critical eyes as he stood in front of him.

"I can tell you exactly," Alister McCraig said. "Mama is very transparent in all her intrigues."

He paused, and as the Duke did not speak, he went on:

"She has told Great-Uncle Hector that I shall doubtless produce a long line of McCraigs, and they must be educated and brought up in the right way, so that they can be a credit to the Clan McCraig."

"Good Lord! So that is her angle!" The Duke laughed. "If nothing else, my sister is undoubtedly a clever diplomat."

"She sent me a copy of the last letter she wrote to Great-Uncle Hector," Alister McCraig said, "and it is that which is bringing him hot-footing to London."

"I see . . ." the Duke remarked reflectively. "There are going to be difficulties if The McCraig wishes to take his place at the first Christening!"

"He cannot live forever!" Alister McCraig said peevishly. "And as far as I am concerned, once he has settled some money on me he can die as quickly as possible!"

"Which is, of course, a most admirable sentiment!" the Duke said ironically.

"Oh, for God's sake, Uncle Yvell," Alister Mc-

Craig said in a tone which betrayed his nervousness, "I hope you are not going to start reproaching me."

The Duke did not speak and he went on:

"It has been drummed into me by my father, my mother, and all my other relations, except you, ever since I was a child, that I had to marry someone befitting my station in life; someone who was the right sort of wife for a Chieftain. The idea of it has always made me sick!"

The Duke thought that perhaps here was the answer to why Alister had given Kitty Varden, a Music-Hall Comedienne with a reputation for singing lewder songs than had ever before been heard on a stage, a wedding-ring.

It was, however, obvious that his nephew was on edge, and if he was to have a nervous actress to cope with too the Duke decided to pour oil on waters that looked like they might become somewhat tempestuous.

"I am sure everything is going to be all right," he said soothingly. "Bardsley is a gentleman, the son of a clergyman as it happens, and he will find us exactly the right sort of wife that you should have had."

"I must say he looks as if he has good blood in him," Alister McCraig remarked. "He does not seem like the usual run of actors."

"He is not!" the Duke said briefly.

There was silence for a moment, then he said:

"I think it is absolutely essential that not a word of this arrangement should be spoken of outside this house. You are well aware, Alister, how a tit-bit of this sort could go round the Clubs like wildfire, and it would only be a question of time before The McCraig learnt of it."

"That is true," his nephew answered. "As a matter of fact, I have not even told Kitty of your idea."

"You have not?" the Duke asked in surprise.

Alister McCraig looked uncomfortable.

"I had a feeling that if I did," he said, "she might insist on meeting Great-Uncle Hector herself. Now that she is settled down she has almost forgotten her past and thinks everyone else has too."

The Duke threw back his head and laughed.

"My dear Alister, if you had not told me that I would not have believed it! If Kitty thinks anyone will ever forget those songs she used to sing, she must have lost what brains she had!"

"Kitty is perfectly content being married to me," Alister McCraig said truculently.

"You have only been married a year, my dear boy. Give it time!"

He saw that his words offended his nephew and added quickly:

"You have been very sensible in not telling Kitty what we are doing. Never trust a woman with a secret if you can possibly help it. Besides, as I have already said, the fewer people know, the better! It would be far too good a story not to repeat."

"That is what I thought, Uncle."

"Then keep your mouth shut, and the most important thing will be to persuade our little actress that unless she too is silent she will not be paid."

The Duke glanced at the clock over the mantelpiece and noted that the hands stood at one minute to twelve o'clock.

His nephew followed the direction of his eyes and said quickly:

"I think, Uncle Yvell, it would be best if you saw this woman alone first. You are much cleverer than I am at getting people to do what you want, and I might mess it up."

Without waiting for his Uncle to agree, Alister McCraig moved across the Library.

"I will be in the Morning-Room when you want me," he said as he reached the door, then he was gone.

There was a smile on the Duke's lips as he bent forward to pick up the *Morning Post*.

He had never had much opinion of his nephew and he thought it was typical of him to shirk the interview at the last moment and shift the responsibility onto his shoulders.

At the same time, he was determined if possible to see that Alister was set up for life, and thus unlikely to be an encumbrance upon him in his old age.

'Damn all relations!' he thought. 'They are always an infernal nuisance!"

He glanced down at the paper, wondering as he did so if he had to be tied not only to his nephew but also to The McCraig of McCraig for the next forty-eight hours.

The idea appalled him, as there was in fact a very amusing party being given that night at the house of Mrs. Mary Ann Clarke, who had once been his mistress but was now under the protection of the Commander-in-Chief of the Army.

It would be the sort of party, the Duke reflected, which scandalised and shocked even the easy-going, pleasure-seeking society that centred round Carlton House.

The difficulty would be, of course, to get away.

"Perhaps the old gentleman will retire early," he told himself. "Then I can escape."

He felt almost like a school-boy planning how to play truant, but with a very different end in view!

There was a cynical twist of amusement on the Duke's lips as the door opened.

"Miss Wantage, Your Grace!"

The Duke rose to his feet.

There was a little pause before Shimona entered the room. Then as she came slowly towards him, holding herself proudly, she was aware of how frightened she was.

She had thought when she left home that it would be quite easy to arrive at Ravenstone House and tell the Duke she had been sent by Beau Bardsley.

She had had everything planned in her mind, and it was only when Nanna had found her a hackney-carriage and she set off alone that she began to feel nervous.

Nanna had been far more difficult to convince than the Doctor, and although once again Shimona had not revealed who had offered to pay one thousand guineas, Nanna had been scandalised at the whole idea.

"What would your poor mother say? What would she think?" she kept repeating.

"Mama would wish us to save Papa's life," Shimona answered, "and there is no other way, Nanna."

"There must be! Surely Dr. Lesley can find the money somehow!"

"How could he possibly find one thousand guineas?"

"It isn't right, Miss Shimona! It isn't right that you should leave the house and go off on your own. I've never heard of such a thing!"

"It will only be for two nights, Nanna."

"*Nights?*" Nanna snorted and made the word sound disreputable and ominous.

"I have promised Dr. Lesley," Shimona went on, "that if anything seems wrong I will return home immediately. I shall not be very far away."

"You will give me the address or you don't leave this house," Nanna said firmly.

"Yes, of course," Shimona agreed.

Then she hesitated, for to say she would be staying at Ravenstone House would certainly reveal the fact that she was meeting the Duke of Ravenstone.

She did not think Nanna had ever heard of him, but when she had been behind the curtain in the dressing-room hearing her father, she had remembered him speaking of the Duke in the most disparaging manner to her mother.

"Ravenstone is after that pretty girl who is the *ingénue* in Act II," Shimona heard him say once when he thought she was not listening. "I have warned her, but the silly little fool is mesmerised by him like a rabbit by a snake!"

"She cannot know what His Grace is like," her mother had said in her soft voice.

"She knows and she still does not care!" Beau Bardsley replied. "There is something about that man which hypnotises women, and until he has left them they are not aware of the sort of devil with whom they have become entangled."

"Is he really as bad as that?" Mrs. Bardsley had asked.

"He is worse!" Beau Bardsley had replied. "He is a disgrace to his title, to his blood, to the stock from which he has sprung! I have no use, Annabel, for a man who betrays his own class."

When her father talked like that Shimona did not realise that he might have been in the pulpit for which he had been intended.

But she had always imagined that the Duke would indeed look like a devil, and once to amuse herself she had drawn a caricature of him with horns on his head and a tail showing beneath his coat.

She had not been able to draw his face because she had never seen him, but she had imagined him with slanting eyes, arched eye-brows, a long thin nose, and pointed ears.

All she had listened to, all she had imagined, came back to her mind as she drove through Hyde Park Corner and along Piccadilly toward Berkeley Square.

As the carriage turned up Berkeley Street she had an impulse to tell the cabman to stop and take her home to the safety of Nanna and her sleeping father.

For the first time she realised how little she knew about the world, how ignorant she was of social behaviour!

She had never been to dinner-parties, she had never even helped to entertain people in her own home with the exception of Dr. Lesley, the Parson, and some of the elderly ladies engaged in charitable work from the Church which she and her mother attended on Sundays.

Sunday to Beau was a day of rest and he never accompanied them.

But Shimona knew that she and her mother were an object of curiosity as they walked up the aisle to sit in an inconspicuous pew behind those which were marked with the names of those who paid for them.

"I am saving Papa! I am saving Papa!"

Shimona repeated the words over and over to herself to give herself confidence.

She felt as if her legs were suddenly very weak, and she was conscious that her heart seemed to be fluttering inside her breast in an extraordinary manner as the carriage came to a standstill.

She looked out and saw a large and very impressive house on the north side of the Square.

It was in fact far bigger than Shimona had anticipated, and when she entered the marble Hall with its great carved staircase and alcoves in which stood Grecian statuary, she felt very small and insignificant.

The Butler had led her to a pair of double mahogany doors.

"May I have your name, Madam?"

Shimona had already decided to call herself Wantage. It happened to be a name in a book which she was reading, and she thought it sounded quiet and unimportant, which was what she wished to be.

She had dressed herself with great care.

She had few gowns to choose from and the muslin that had been made by Nanna was very plain, but the cloak which covered it was of a blue which matched her eyes and had been bought for her by her mother.

Her bonnet was high-crowned but not over-fashionable, and the blue ribbons which ornamented it were simple but in perfect taste.

The Butler opened the door.

"Miss Wantage, Your Grace!" he said in a manner which made Shimona feel as if he had blown a fanfare.

Then she remembered that for the first time she was to meet face to face the man she had thought of as a devil.

Almost instinctively, as if she was taking part in a play, she paused as the door shut behind her.

She looked across the room and she saw not the devil she had anticipated, but an extremely good-looking man, who was surprisingly young for his reputation.

He was by no means as handsome as her father,

nor were his features in the least classical, and yet he
was outstandingly distinguished-looking and had a
natural grace and elegance which Shimona knew derived from his breeding.

He also stood looking at her, taking in the little
pointed face under the plain bonnet, the slim figure
in a muslin gown, and the wide, dark blue eyes that
looked at him questioningly.

He had expected that Beau Bardsley would send
him someone attractive, but not a woman so exquisite-
ly beautiful.

In fact she was so inexpressibly lovely that,
cynical and satiated though he was with all the de-
lights that the female sex could offer him, the Duke was
for the moment speechless.

Slowly, very slowly, Shimona advanced towards
him. Then almost as if he remembered his manners, he
moved towards her.

"You come, I think, from Mr. Beau Bardsley?"

With an effort and in a voice which did not sound
like her own Shimona managed to reply:

"Y-yes . . . Your Grace."

She curtseyed and felt as she did so that it was
a relief to be able to take her eyes from his.

The Duke bowed.

"I am very grateful to you, Miss Wantage. Will
you not be seated?"

"Thank . . . you."

Shimona sat down on the edge of a chair beside
the fire and looked at him with eyes in which to his
surprise he could see an unmistakable expression
of fear.

"You must not be frightened," he said in the voice
which she had last heard from behind the curtain in
her father's dressing-room. "I know this may be an un-
usual part for you to play, but I am quite certain you
will do it most admirably!"

"Thank . . . you."

"Have you been on the stage long?" the Duke
asked, seating himself. "I cannot remember ever having seen you in a play."

He thought even as he spoke that it was an idiotic question.

If he had once seen this beautiful creature behind the footlights it would have been impossible for him not only to forget her, but to have failed to try to make her acquaintance.

Shimona glanced at him for a moment, then she said:

"Will you ... tell me ... Your Grace ... exactly what is ... required of me?"

The Duke smiled.

"What you are really saying, Miss Wantage, is that you have no wish to answer questions about yourself."

"I did not ... mean to be ... impertinent ... Your Grace."

"You are not. I do not think you could be," he replied.

There was an expression in his eyes which made Shimona look away from him.

She wished that her heart were not pounding so wildly, almost as if it would burst from her breast, and she was ashamed of the fact that her hands were still trembling.

"It is warm in here," the Duke said unexpectedly. "I think you would be wise to remove your cloak, and I am sure you would be more comfortable without your bonnet."

"Y-yes ... of course."

Shimona rose to her feet like a child obedient to a command.

She unclasped her cloak at the neck and the Duke took it from her.

He came close to her to do so, and she had a strange feeling. It was not one of panic, but something very like it which she could not explain to herself.

As the Duke laid her cloak on a chair against a wall, she undid the ribbons of her bonnet and he took that also.

"You have brought enough clothes with you for two nights?" he asked.

"Yes . . . Your Grace."

He came back to the fireside and resumed his seat.

Shimona sat opposite him.

The light from the flames shone on her fair hair, and yet it still held the mysterious shadows that Richard Cosway had painted so skilfully in the miniature of her mother.

Her eyes, the Duke thought, were the blue of a stormy sea and not the pale colour one would have expected with such white skin. Her nose reminded him of the statuary he had seen when he had last been in Greece.

He realised she was waiting for him to speak and after a moment he said:

"Beau Bardsley doubtless will have told you that my nephew could inherit a very large sum of money if his Great-Uncle, The McCraig of McCraig, likes his wife, to whom he has been married for a year."

Shimona was listening intently and he went on:

"He has in fact told his mother, who is a widow, and his Great-Uncle very little about the woman he has married, which makes it easy for you to play the part."

"Do they know her name?" Shimona asked.

"They have been told her real name, which is Katherine Webber," the Duke replied, "but not the one she used professionally. You will of course be called Katherine while you are here."

Shimona acquiesced with a little inclination of her head.

"What is your Christian name, Miss Wantage?" the Duke asked.

"Shimona!"

As she spoke she thought it might have been wiser to call herself Mary or Jane.

"I have never before known anyone called Shimona," he remarked.

"I must . . . remember to answer to . . . Katherine."

"Of course, and my nephew will tell you anything

it is necessary for you to know about his wife."

As he mentioned Alister McCraig, the Duke noticed that Shimona glanced towards the door as if she expected someone overpowering or even menacing to enter the room.

"You will not feel nervous with Alister," he said soothingly. "He is an easy-going, charming young man. In fact the only person whom you need fear at all will be The McCraig himself."

"Why is he called The McCraig of McCraig?" Shimona asked.

"It is a title which some Clans give their Chieftains and of which they are very proud. It gives them the standing of an Earl or perhaps a Marquess in this country, and I am certain The McCraig would not change it for any other title, however distinguished."

"I have read about the Clan McCraig in the history of Scotland," Shimona said.

"You are interested in history?"

"I love it!" she answered.

"Why?" the Duke enquired.

Shimona thought for a moment. She was used to answering her father's questions seriously, so she replied:

"I suppose because it shows us the evolution of civilisation. I particularly enjoy the history of Greece."

"You look like a Greek goddess yourself," the Duke remarked. "But I expect many men have told you that."

To his astonishment, his words brought the colour flaming into Shimona's cheeks and her eyes dropped before his.

It was in fact the first compliment she had ever been paid by a man other than her father or the Doctor.

"We were ... speaking of the ... task which lies ahead of ... me, Your Grace," she managed to say after a moment or two.

"Yes, of course," the Duke agreed.

Then as if he could not help himself he asked:

"Surely you are very young to be on the stage? There must be something better you could do!"

Shimona looked at him with a worried expression in her eyes, and he knew that she was not going to give him a truthful answer.

Chapter Three

The dinner was coming to an end and Shimona had been entranced with everything about it.

She had never imagined a Dining-Room could look so attractive or that a table could be literally groaning under gold ornaments and candelabra.

It was also tastefully decorated with flowers, and as she sampled dish after dish served on gold plate by powdered flunkeys, she felt as if she was acting a part on the stage.

"And that is exactly what I am doing!" she told herself.

At the same time, she had had no idea, she thought, that the props and the scenery would be so magnificent!

The McCraig of McCraig had not in fact been as frightening as she had anticipated.

She knew that he was eighty years of age, but he certainly did not look it, for he held himself stiffly upright and there was an inescapable dignity about him which Shimona thought must win respect wherever he went.

He looked, with his high-bridged nose, his white hair swept back from his square forehead, his shrewd eyes under bushy eye-brows, exactly how she thought a Chieftain should look.

As the evening progressed she could not help wondering how Alister McCraig could have married a somewhat disreputable actress when he had so much history behind him and such distinguished fore-bears.

Both the Duke and Alister realised that The Mc-

Craig was agreeably impressed by Shimona from the moment he saw her.

It would in fact have been hard for him not to do so. As she curtseyed to him, her grace had reminded the Duke of the swans on his lake at Ravenstone.

But while she bore herself proudly there was no mistaking the touch of fear in her eyes and the worried look on her lovely face, which perceptively the Duke thought pleased the old Scot.

After all, he told himself, The McCraig was expecting not only an ill-bred actress, which Kitty undoubtedly was, but also someone who might be pert and aggressive simply because she would think he was condescending to her.

But Shimona actually played no part except that of being herself, striking just the right note of respect without being obsequious.

Luncheon was announced soon after The McCraig had arrived, and he talked of his journey South to the Duke while at the same time, they all knew, watching Shimona from under his thick eye-brows.

"I have an appointment with the Prime Minister," he said as luncheon was ending, "at half after two."

"I will order a carriage for you," the Duke remarked.

"That will leave you two young people free for an hour or so," The McCraig said to his great-nephew and Shimona.

"What would you wish to do?" the Duke enquired.

He thought with a faint air of amusement that the answer was all too obvious.

What woman, especially from the world of the theatre, could resist such an opportunity to spend money? He waited with a mocking look in his eyes for Shimona's answer.

She was, however, looking across the table at The McCraig.

"Would it be . . . possible, Sir," she enquired, "if you are . . . visiting the Prime Minister, for me to . . . see the House of Commons?"

"I am sure it could be arranged," The McCraig answered. "You are interested in politics?"

"I read the Parliamentary reports every day in the *Times*," Shimona replied, "and I have been deeply distressed by the reports of the Highland evictions."

As she spoke she wondered if she had been indiscreet. The McCraig might be one of the landlords who were prepared to evict their own people to make the land nothing but a sheep-walk.

But fortunately she had struck the right note.

"I am glad you feel like that," The McCraig said. "It is a gross injustice, a betrayal of our own flesh and blood, and those who perpetrate such atrocities should be shot!"

He spoke with a violence which seemed to boom out in the Dining-Room.

Then he talked for ten minutes of the sufferings of the Highlanders, who, uprooted from all that was familiar, had been transported to Canada and other parts of the world, without even adequate provision being made for them when they arrived.

"I do not expect," he said at length, "to find much understanding and sympathy amongst the Sassenachs, but I might have known that your husband, being a McCraig, would have made you realise the iniquity of what is happening in the North."

He beamed at his great-nephew as he spoke and luncheon ended in an atmosphere of mellow good humour.

The Duke's carriage conveyed The McCraig with Alister and Shimona to the House of Commons, and arrangements were made on their arrival for them to be shown to the Strangers' Gallery.

They sat there for over an hour until they were notified that The McCraig had finished his business with the Prime Minister.

He was in somewhat of a bad temper when they joined him because the Hon. Henry Addington, who had replaced the brilliant William Pitt, was a weak man who found it hard to make a decision.

He was obviously not prepared to agree to implement the reforms which The McCraig advocated.

But as they drove back to Berkeley Square
Shimona managed to coax the old gentleman back into
a good humour, which continued until it was time to
change for dinner.

The bed-room she was to use at Ravenstone
House was, Shimona thought, almost as impressive as
the rooms downstairs.

Her mother had taught her to appreciate beautiful furniture and she exclaimed with delight over
the French commodes in her bed-room, just as she
was longing, when she had time, to inspect the ex-
quisitely carved Charles II gilt tables which ornamented the Salon.

There were two maids to wait on her and she
enjoyed the hot bath prepared with jasmine which
was set in front of the fire, and the lavender-scented
towels with which she could dry herself.

She kept wishing she could tell her mother all
about the house, then wondered if her mother, like
her father, would be very angry at her being a guest of
the Duke.

There was something about him which was def-
initely frightening, she thought, and yet at the same
time she found it hard not to admire him.

It was not only because of his good looks, it was
also the way he walked, as if he owned the whole
world, and his air of distinction.

She found herself thinking continually that the
house and its contents were a fitting background for
him.

"Why does he shock people so much?" she asked
herself. "And why does Papa say that he behaves
like a devil?"

The Duke's manners were impeccable and she
knew that he was trying in every possible way to
prevent her from feeling embarrassed or anxious at
any question which The McCraig put to her.

She realised it was for his own ends, and yet it
was impossible, where she was concerned, not to think
of him as being kind and considerate.

When she went downstairs holding on to the bannister of the carved staircase, she felt an irrepressible little thrill of excitement at the prospect of spending the evening with the Duke.

She had glanced at her reflection in the mirror before she left her bed-room and thought that Alister McCraig would not be ashamed to own her as his wife.

Because she thought it made her look older she was wearing one of her mother's evening-gowns.

It was a deep blue which matched the eyes of both of them, and there was a shimmer of silver beneath the soft gauze with which it was made, and sprinkled in the tulle which framed the bodice there were tiny dew-drops of diamonds.

It was the sort of elaborate gown which could have been worn to a Ball or a Reception, and yet no-one but Beau Bardsley had ever seen it.

"Why do you buy such elaborate gowns, Mama, when you never go out, but only dine at home with Papa?" Shimona had asked.

Her mother had hesitated for a moment before she replied:

"It is difficult to explain, dearest, but your father meets many beautiful women, not only in the theatre but also when he is invited to the houses of the nobility."

She gave a little sigh.

"I am not included in the invitations, but I wish him to see me looking my best, as I would if I could accompany him."

There was something pathetic in the words, which made Shimona say quickly:

"You always look beautiful, Mama, whatever you wear. Papa has often said that to him you are the most beautiful woman in the whole world!"

"I want him always to think so," Mrs. Bardsley said softly, "and that is why I dress to please him."

Shimona had understood, but because there was often a shortage of money, the elaborate gowns were not as many as her mother would have wished.

Nevertheless, as they had been kept so carefully, there was, now that her mother was dead, quite a number for Shimona to choose from.

That her choice was a good one she knew as soon as she entered the Salon.

The three men were waiting for her by the fire-place, and as she moved towards them she found it impossible for her eyes not to seek the Duke's. There was an expression in his that she knew she had wanted to see.

The conversation at dinner proved even more interesting than it had been at luncheon.

The McCraig talked of the difficulties in the Highlands and the Duke talked of sport.

Because Shimona listened wide-eyed and with interest to everything that was said, they drew her into the conversation and explained to her all she did not understand.

Now as dinner finished she looked a little nervously at the Duke and asked:

"Should I . . . retire and leave you to your port?"

Her mother had told her that this is what happened at the end of a formal dinner and the Duke smiled as if she had done the right thing.

As they all rose to their feet he said:

"We will not be long."

Shimona went from the Dining-Room down the passage to the Salon.

A flunkey opened the door and as soon as she was alone she started to examine the treasures which the room contained.

There was so much to see, so much to admire, that she was in fact quite surprised when the gentlemen joined her.

She turned as they entered, holding in her hand a miniature of a lovely woman which had been lying on one of the tables amongst a collection of snuff-boxes.

The Duke came to her side.

"I see you are admiring one of my miniatures," he said. "I have a large collection in another room."

"I am sure this is by Richard Cosway."

"It is a portrait of my mother."

"Oh, how strange, he also painted mine!" Shimona exclaimed.

As she spoke she wondered if she had made a mistake, but The McCraig had walked to the fireplace and was talking to his great-nephew.

"That is another thing we have in common," the Duke said in a low voice.

"Another?" Shimona questioned.

"There are many—we both love beauty, for one."

"Yes . . . yes, of course."

She did not know why, but she found it difficult to talk naturally when he was standing so near to her.

There was also a note in his voice which made her vibrate just as she and the audience would vibrate to her father's voice on the stage.

Because she felt shy she put down the miniature and walked towards the fireplace.

The McCraig looked at her from under his eyebrows and said:

"I have been thinking that you have been extremely kind in listening to an old man talking about his hobby-horses ever since I arrived. Tomorrow you must tell me something about yourself."

"Everything you have said, Sir, has been so interesting," Shimona answered. "I feel that anything I could relate would pale into insignificance."

The McCraig smiled.

"You are too modest," he said. "But there has been enough talking for tonight. You will, I know, excuse me if I go to bed. I am used to early hours and I have travelled a long way."

"I am sure you must be weary, Sir," Alister said.

The McCraig turned to the Duke.

"Good-night, Ravenstone. I am enjoying your hospitality and thank you for it."

"It is a very great pleasure," the Duke replied.

The McCraig touched Shimona on the shoulder and smiled at her.

"I shall look forward to our talk tomorrow."

He walked across the Salon with his shoulders

back and his head held high while Alister hurried
after him to escort him to the foot of the staircase.

The Duke and Shimona were left alone.

"You have been very clever with him," the Duke
said approvingly.

"I think he is a very charming old man," Shimona
answered, "and so interesting."

"Were you really interested in his tales of Scotland? Or was that part of the act?"

"Of course I was interested!" Shimona replied
indignantly. "Who could fail to be?"

"And you enjoyed visiting the House of Commons?"

"It was thrilling! I have imagined so often what it
was like, but hearing the speeches and seeing the
Members sitting on the benches was quite different
from what I expected."

"Different?"

"They were so . . . casual about it," Shimona explained, feeling for words. "Sprawling with their feet
up, their hats tipped over their eyes, and half the time
no-one seemed to be listening!"

"That is the way we are governed," the Duke said,
smiling.

"Perhaps that is how democracy should be," she
said reflectively, "not regimented, but at ease until one
is galvanised into fighting for something that is really
worthwhile!"

The Duke looked at her in surprise, but before he
could speak Alister joined them.

"God, but you were magnificent!" he exclaimed to
Shimona. "You have the old man eating out of your
hand. I would never have credited that a woman
could be so clever!"

There was something about his enthusiasm which
jarred on Shimona.

She turned to look at the fire, feeling somehow
as if he made her feel cheap and a fraud.

"What are the plans for tomorrow?" the Duke
asked.

"There is a Military Parade which he wishes to attend in Hyde Park in the morning," Alister replied. "Apparently one of the Scottish Regiments is taking part. In the afternoon he proposes to visit Kew Gardens."

The Duke laughed.

"I can see you are in for a riot of fun and gaiety!"

"Am I to go with you?" Shimona asked.

"I am afraid you will have to," Alister replied.

"Oh, I am glad!" she cried. "It sounds so exciting, and I have never seen a Military Parade."

"I will make arrangements for you all to be at the saluting base," the Duke said.

"You will not be able to come with us?" Shimona asked. "How disappointing for you!"

"Indeed it is most regrettable, but I have a previous engagement," the Duke replied, and his eyes were twinkling.

"Please come with us in the afternoon, Uncle Yvell," Alister pleaded. "You know a lot about gardens because of the fine ones at Ravenstone, but I can hardly tell one flower from another."

"Then I see I shall have to sacrifice myself," the Duke replied. "Would you like to tell Captain Graham of our intentions so that he can make arrangements regarding the carriages and of course the seats at the Military Parade?"

"I will tell him at once," Alister agreed. "He will not have gone to bed?"

"Captain Graham never goes to bed," the Duke answered, and his nephew laughed.

"I am sure that is true. Who except a superman could be Comptroller of your Household?"

He walked away and the Duke said in explanation to Shimona:

"Captain Graham is my secretary and general factotum. You will find he can procure everything you want, everything you need, and, if necessary, at a moment's notice, arrange a journey to the moon!"

"I have no wish to visit the moon," Shimona answered. "It always looks such a cold and empty place. One of the twinkling stars would be far more exciting!"

"That is what you have been the whole evening," the Duke replied. "A twinkling star. Do I have to tell you that you have been quite wonderful?"

Her eyes dropped before his and she said a little incoherently:

"I think . . . Your Grace . . . it is time for me to . . . retire to bed."

"So early?" the Duke questioned. "Would you not wish to dance, to seek some of the many amusements with which London abounds?"

"No, no, of course not," Shimona replied quickly, thinking how horrified her father would be. "Your Grace will understand that like The McCraig I also am . . . tired."

"You do not like to dance?"

Shimona was just about to say that she had never been to a dance. Then she remembered that would not be in keeping with the actress she was supposed to be.

"It is . . . sometimes very . . . pleasant," she said after a moment.

"But you do not wish to dance either with Alister or me?" the Duke persisted.

There was a perceptible pause before Shimona replied:

"I think, Your Grace, it would be a mistake for me to be seen in . . . public with Mr. McCraig when many people must be . . . aware that he is . . . married."

The Duke smiled as if he realised she had thought up the excuse.

"You are a very strange person," he said slowly, "and I am being completely honest when I say quite unlike anyone I have ever met before."

She looked up at him to see if he was mocking her, then found it hard to look away.

"Tell me the truth. Are you really looking forward to seeing a Military Parade tomorrow and going to Kew Gardens?"

"I especially want to see Kew Gardens again," Shimona said in a low voice, "I have not been there since . . ."

She stopped.

She had been about to say that she had not been there since her mother's death. Then she wondered if it was a mistake to say too much about herself.

She did not realise how expressive her eyes were.

"You have not been there since you were with someone who mattered a great deal to you," the Duke said.

Shimona did not reply. She was thinking how unexpectedly perceptive he was.

"Who was that person?" he enquired, and there was a note in his voice that she did not understand.

Because she felt compelled to answer him she said:

"My . . . mother."

"And she is dead?"

"Yes. She . . . died two years . . . ago."

"And you loved her very much?"

"More than I can ever say."

"But you have other members of your family?"

"Yes . . ."

Shimona felt embarrassed by his interrogation and glanced towards the door. But there was no sign of Alister McCraig.

"May I . . . retire, Your Grace?"

"Are you running away from me or from my questions?"

"Perhaps . . . both, Your Grace."

"But you are not so afraid of me as you were when you arrived?"

She looked at him in surprise. She had hoped he had not realised how frightened she had been.

Unexpectedly she smiled.

"I am still frightened . . . Your Grace, but now my legs will support me and my heart has stopped turning . . . somersaults."

He laughed.

"The question I would like to ask you," he said

after a moment, "is whether you judge people by what you have heard about them, or by what you yourself feel?"

Shimona tried to find words with which to answer him. Then before she could do so Alister McCraig came back into the Salon.

"Everything is arranged," he said, "and now, if you will forgive me, Uncle Yvell, I am going back to Kitty.

"I told her I had to be with you to discuss financial matters with your Attorneys. She knew I would remain for dinner, but she will certainly not expect me to stay the night."

"Very well, Alister," the Duke replied, "but you had best be back in time to breakfast with your Great-Uncle."

"I will not be late, that I promise you," Alister answered. "I certainly do not wish to disrupt the excellent impression our brilliant little actress has made on him!"

Once again Shimona felt that his words were slightly degrading.

She curtseyed low to the Duke, but not so low to her supposed husband.

"Good-night, Your Grace. Good-night, Mr. McCraig."

Then she went quickly from the Salon before they could escort her.

* * *

Driving towards the party which the Duke had expected he might have to miss that evening, he thought how simply and without a hitch everything had proceeded.

He had imagined that all sorts of difficulties might arise when the McCraig met his great-nephew's supposed wife, but there was no doubt that Shimona had swept away his opposition and any feeling of aggression he may have had from the very first moment.

She was in fact, the Duke told himself, the most amazing actress he had ever encountered—if indeed she was acting.

He had asked Beau Bardsley for a lady and Beau had certainly provided him with one.

There was good breeding, the Duke thought, not only in Shimona's exquisite features, but also in her long fingers, her arched insteps, and in every word she spoke.

Hers was not the assumed accent of a "Lady of Quality" which he had heard so often on the stage, nor had she any need to pick and choose her words.

She was as natural as a flower, and that, he thought, was what she resembled: the purity of a lily, perhaps a rose still in bud, or again the syringa blossoms which scented the gardens at Ravenstone in the spring.

"Good God, I am becoming a sentimentalist!" he told himself, and tried to concentrate on Mary Ann Clarke.

He had in fact, when he had grown bored, introduced her to His Royal Highness.

Mary Ann at twenty-seven was not only extremely attractive, she also loved life and bubbled over with a gaiety which was all her own.

"If anyone can make H.R.H. forget his frigid, ugly, German wife, his Army duties and money difficulties, it is Mrs. Clarke," an Officer under his Command had remarked.

Established by her Royal protector in a large Mansion in Gloucester Place with twenty servants including three coachmen, and three Chefs, Mary Ann was making the most of her new position.

At her parties she supplied her guests, the Bucks and Blades of St. James's, with beautiful girls of every colour and led her Royal protector into wild excesses.

It was of course expected that every Gentleman of Fashion should have a mistress, and despite the sanctimonious boredom of the Court at Buckingham House it was a robust, bawdy, promiscuous age.

The rowdy parties and the very undesirable friends the Prince of Wales collected round him came in for a lot of criticism; anything which happened at

Carlton House was mild compared with the orgies that took place in other noblemen's houses.

A large number of His Royal Highness's closest friends were certain to be at Mary Ann's this evening.

They would include the two most notorious Dukes in England, Queensbury and Norfolk, both of them celebrated drunkards and the former a dedicated lecher.

Sir John Wade, an amazing disreputable figure who derived a large fortune from a brewery, was sure to be another guest. His wife had numbered the Duke of York among her lovers.

Thinking of the fair charmers with whom he had spent many amusing hours before he tired of them, the Duke's mind lingered on Fanny Norton.

The daughter of a dressmaker in Southampton, after many protectors including Richard Brinsley Sheridan and himself, she had been sold by Colonel Harvey Aston, a leading light of the Quorn Hunt, when he was hard up for five hundred guineas, to the Earl of Barrymore.

A doubtful exchange, as nicknamed "Hellgate" because of his violent temper, he was one of the most debauched men in London.

The Duke remembered how Fanny had been led on a silken halter into Colonel Aston's Dining-Room, where he was presiding over a stag-party which included "Hellgate."

She wore only a single garment, giving His Lordship every chance of seeing what he was getting for his money.

Buying a mistress had become quite a vogue.

When he was young the Duke of York had bought one of his first mistresses, the daughter of an hautboy player, for fifteen hundred guineas.

Lord Hervey's doxy was a tiny, doll-like creature called Vanelle Vane and the Prime Minister also fancied her. Lord Hervey made her over to him for a generous sum.

'Thank God I have never needed to buy a woman!' the Duke thought to himself as his carriage travelled towards Gloucester Place.

He could not blind himself to the fact that they rushed into his arms before he even signified any interest in them.

But he was, as they all knew, extremely generous to those whom he took under his protection, although unfortunately he was also known to tire of them very easily, and any pretty Cyprian he fancied soon found herself looking round for another banker.

Nevertheless, the Duke thought, these pretty, expendable "bits o' muslin" could be amusing if only for a short time.

The carriage was crossing Oxford Street and looking out through the window the Duke saw on the pavement a ragged man selling a publication which was greatly in demand by those who could not afford to set up their own establishments.

It was called *The Whoremongers Guide to London* and contained addresses of Houses of Pleasure and descriptions of those known as the "Covent Garden Nuns."

There were as usual a number of street-walkers standing near the lamps which illuminated quite effectively the more-frequented thoroughfares. Some of them looked very young and were in fact little more than children.

Their eyes were painted, their lips reddened, and there was no mistaking the eagerness with which they tried to accost every male passer-by.

As the carriage drove on quite suddenly the Duke had no wish for the type of entertainment which he knew was waiting for him in Gloucester Place.

He unexpectedly felt bored at the thought of Mary Ann Clarke's exuberance and the simulated professional gaiety of the girls she would have chosen with such care.

He found himself thinking of two worried blue eyes and a soft voice which had a note of fear behind it.

The Duke bent forward and rapped with his gold-handled cane on the front of the carriage behind the coachman.

The horses were drawn to a standstill and the footman jumped down to open the door.

"White's Club!" the Duke ordered.

As the horses were turned round and started back the way they had come he said to himself in a tone of astonishment:

"Good God! I must be getting old!"

* * *

The afternoon was as sunny as it had been in the morning. The air was crisp but it was warm for late October, and Shimona had discarded her blue cloak and was quite warm enough in the jacket which covered her gown.

She had found the Military Parade in the morning as exciting as she had anticipated, and when the Scottish Regiment marched past, led by the pipe band, her eyes had been shining and she seemed so thrilled that The McCraig had looked at her with approval.

"I never believed that men could appear so magnificent as they do in the kilt," she told The McCraig as they drove back to Berkeley Square.

"You and your husband must come and stay at Castle Craig, then you can see and hear my own pipers," The McCraig replied.

The words made her feel as if dowsed with cold water.

With an effort Shimona remembered that she would never be taken to stay at the Castle nor would she hear The McCraig's pipers.

As if he sensed her sudden embarrassment, Alister said quickly:

"I remember hearing your pipers when I was a small boy, Great-Uncle. I used to creep out of bed when we stayed at the Castle to hear them going round the table at dinner and longed to be downstairs."

"Well, you are old enough to enjoy them now,"

The McCraig replied, "and when you have a son of your own you must teach him the history of the McCraigs and how well they fought in battle, marching behind their own pipers."

"I shall do that," Alister said, and there was no doubt of his sincerity.

The McCraig had looked at Shimona.

"I do not wish to make you blush," he said, "but I would like to see my great-grand-nephew before I die."

His words did make Shimona blush and she was thankful when the carriage came to a standstill in Berkeley Square.

Luncheon was a small meal compared to the large dinner they had eaten the night before, and Shimona wondered whether the Duke's slim, athletic figure was due to the fact that he ate little and took a large amount of exercise.

She had learnt from Alister that his appointment that morning had not been of a very serious nature, but that he always rode for several hours in the Park schooling the horses which his grooms found too hard to handle.

As soon as luncheon was finished they set off for Kew Gardens, and now at the Duke's suggestion they travelled in two Phaetons, he tooling one and Alister the other.

Both Phaetons had a groom up behind, but Shimona found herself to all intents and purposes alone with the Duke.

She did not pretend to herself that it was not something that she wished for and enjoyed.

She had known last night, when she thought over what had happened during the day, that what she most notably remembered were her conversations with the Duke.

When he was present, she thought, it was difficult for her to notice anyone else or even attend to any conversation in which he did not take part.

She could not understand this, except that she realised he had the same kind of magnetism that her father had, a power to draw people to him and to hold them spellbound.

Never before, she thought as they drove along, had the sun seemed so golden or the day held a magic which it was difficult to put into words.

"You are warm enough?" the Duke asked as the horses moved more quickly when they were free of the heavy traffic in Piccadilly.

"I am very warm," Shimona replied. "It is such a lovely day!"

She looked up at the sky as she spoke and the Duke glanced at her perfect profile and the long line of her neck before his attention returned to his horses.

"One day," he said, "I must show you my garden in the country. It was laid out by my grandfather when he made many alterations to the house and he employed the great gardeners of the time."

"Let me guess who they were," Shimona said. "Charles Bridgeman, William Kent, and Capability Brown."

"You are very knowledgeable, Miss Wantage, and completely correct in your assumption."

"Have you any of the William Kent furniture?"

"Several pairs of tables," the Duke replied.

"Oh, I would love to see them!" Shimona exclaimed.

"I want to show them to you."

She was just about to ask more about them when she remembered that she would never have a chance of seeing the Duke's gardens or his furniture.

Tomorrow morning she would disappear out of his life as unceremoniously as she had come into it.

Never, never must her father guess where she had been or what she had done!

She was already trying to concoct a story to explain how they now had enough money to go abroad.

Dr. Lesley would help her there, she hoped, and Nanna had promised never to disclose that she had been away from the house in Chelsea for two nights.

At least Nanna had not known where she had gone, because, although she had insisted on having

Shimona's address, it had in fact been placed in an envelope which Nanna had sworn she would not open except in an emergency.

"If Papa becomes dangerously ill and Dr. Lesley tells you to send for me, then open the envelope," Shimona instructed her.

"I don't like all this secrecy," Nanna said fiercely. "If your mother's looking down from Heaven at us— God rest her soul!—she would say the same!"

"Mama would want us to save Papa," Shimona repeated for the thousandth time.

But Nanna was still grumbling when she left the house.

"Nothing matters except that Papa should get well," Shimona told herself now.

At the same time, she was conscious of something almost like a little ache in her heart at the thought that she would never see the Duke again—never again see his handsome face, or hear his voice with that particular note in it that always made her feel a little breathless.

She had been aware that he looked at her admiringly when she came into the Salon before luncheon, having removed the bonnet she had worn for the Military Parade, to find him having a glass of sherry with The McCraig.

It had been an effort to walk across the room towards him, and yet at the same time it was difficult to prevent herself from running to reach him.

"What are you thinking about?" he asked now, breaking in on her thoughts.

"I was thinking about your house in the country. Is it very large?"

"Very large, very impressive, and I think very beautiful!" he replied laughingly.

"Then it must be," she answered, "because you have such good taste."

He turned to look at her fleetingly and she saw that his eye-brows were raised.

"Was that rude?" she asked quickly. "Should I not have said it?"

"It is a compliment which I accept with great pleasure!"

Shimona thought for a moment, then she said:

"But you are surprised that an . . . actress should recognise good taste."

"I did not say so."

"But that is what you thought."

"The truth is that I am afraid of your reading my thoughts so easily."

"As I . . . am when you read . . . mine."

"You have something to hide and you are in fact hiding it from me very successfully."

There was silence until, when they had driven further, the Duke said:

"I wish that you would trust me, even though there is little reason why you should do so."

Shimona laughed.

"I . . . want to trust you . . . and I hate having . . . secrets . . . it is very . . . difficult . . ."

"I have a feeling, although I may be mistaken, that you find it hard to lie."

"I have never lied!" Shimona said quickly. "Except . . ."

"Except at this moment?"

Shimona made a gesture with her hands.

"Please . . ." she pleaded, "you are making it very . . . difficult and I am doing what you want."

"And doing it brilliantly," the Duke said in a low voice. "So much so that I am not only astonished and bewildered, but also intrigued and most curious!"

Shimona sat staring straight ahead of her.

The sun glinted on the silver of the horses' harness and it seemed to dazzle her eyes, or was it that she was dazzled by the man beside her?

They reached Kew Gardens and Alister, who had been following close behind, drew up his horses near to them.

It was obvious as soon as they began to walk round the gardens that The McCraig was very knowledgeable about plants and shrubs, especially about those that had recently been discovered.

Alister never said a word, and as the old man seemed content to talk to Shimona, the Duke also relapsed into silence.

"Discovering a new plant is just as exciting, if not more so, than discovering a new planet," The McCraig said.

"You are thinking of Uranus, Sir," Shimona smiled. "I have read how it was discovered by Sir William Herschel, who was a musician before becoming an astronomer."

"That is right!" The McCraig said, obviously delighted at her knowledge. "And I expect you know that it was David Douglas who brought the Douglas Fir from the West Coast of America."

"I am afraid I am more interested in flowers, Sir," Shimona said, "which my mother loved. She told me how excited she was when she first saw the gold lily—*lycoris*—when she was a little girl."

"A beautiful bloom," The McCraig said. "But I prefer the Fuchsia, which was introduced only a few years ago and which I can grow in Scotland."

"I can understand that," Shimona smiled.

They looked at the Chinese Pagoda and at the Chinese gardens round it, which were of particular interest to The McCraig.

"Do you know anything about the Chinese?" he asked Shimona.

"I know they have ancient medicines which they have found efficacious over the centuries," she replied.

"Medicines?" he queried.

"All flowers and plants have medicinal qualities."

"I know there are herbs used by the gypsies and some country folk," the Duke interposed, "but are you telling me that ordinary flowers can be used medicinally?"

Shimona smiled at him.

"Of course they can! Roses, for instance, to help the heart and liver, and not only to prevent pain but also heal internal wounds."

"I never realised that before!" the Duke exclaimed.

"The lily-of-the-valley is particularly good for rheumatism and depression and also helps the brain."

"Then I can think of a number of acquaintances who need that," the Duke remarked drily.

"Have you made a study of this?" The McCraig enquired.

"My mother was very interested in herbs and flowers and she taught me quite a lot about them," Shimona replied simply.

"Your wife is far more talented and knowledgeable than I ever expected in anyone so young," The McCraig said to Alister as they walked back through the Gardens to where their Phaetons were waiting.

"I am a very lucky man!" he said lightly.

"You are indeed! Very lucky!" The McCraig answered, and there was no doubt that he meant it.

As they drove back in the Phaeton the Duke said:

"Once again you have given a performance that was not only faultless but would bring any audience to their feet!"

"It was not a .. performance!"

"I realise that."

"We are lying to him about only one thing," Shimona said. "Surely therefore what we are doing cannot be so very . . . wrong?"

She was pleading with him almost like a child who wishes to be reassured, and after a moment the Duke said:

"I do not think that anyone would consider it wrong to make the old gentleman happy, which he obviously is in your company, and to allay his fears where his great-nephew is concerned."

"But if he ever finds out?" Shimona asked.

"That is something which must not happen! Alister made a monumental mistake in marrying this woman, but I do not wish him to be penalised for the rest of his life."

The Duke spoke almost harshly.

"Would you . . . feel that about any . . . actress he had married?" Shimona enquired.

"If he had married someone like you I should have been delighted, as obviously The McCraig is, that he had found anyone so exceptional."

"But at the same time you think that a man should not . . . marry out of his own . . . position in life."

There was a pause before the Duke answered:

"I will not insult your intelligence by denying that I think marriage should be between two people who are born equally."

"Then what you are saying is that it is what a man *is*, rather than what he *does*, which counts?" Shimona argued.

The Duke drove on a little way before he replied:

"You are pushing me into a corner out of which I find it difficult to extricate myself. What you are really asking is this: If a gentleman, like Beau Bardsley, and a lady, such as you obviously are, are on the stage, is that of more importance than the class in which they were born?"

"Yes," Shimona said in a low voice. "That is what I am . . . trying to say."

"It depends on what they want of life," the Duke answered. "If they are content with the plaudits of the crowd, if they want professional success and fame, then the fact that they are not accepted as the equal of those who consider themselves of social importance cannot be of any consequence to them."

Shimona did not reply, then he said:

"I have a feeling, however, it would always be of consequence to a woman."

He turned to look at her before he added:

"I have already asked you if there is not something more worthwhile and more suitable you can do than to be an actress."

Chapter Four

The gentlemen came into the Salon where Shimona was once again looking at the *objets d'art*.

She turned with a smile and The McCraig said:

"Come here, Katherine. I want to speak to you and Alister."

He spoke seriously and Shimona gave the Duke a little worried glance before obediently she followed the old man to the hearth-rug.

He stood with his back to the fire and as Shimona and Alister joined him he said:

"I understand that the Duke has been kind enough to accommodate you here in his house while you look for one of your own. I am sure you appreciate his generosity. At the same time, I know that it is important for you both to have a home."

He paused and Shimona wondered what he was going to say.

"I have thought it over . . ." he continued, "and I realise that Alister cannot afford at the moment to buy a house which would be a proper background for his wife, and in the future a family."

Shimona saw that Alister was listening intently and there was a faint smile on his lips as if he anticipated what was to come.

"I have therefore decided," The McCraig went on, "that when I return to Scotland I will settle a sum of money on my great-nephew which will enable him to live comfortably as befits his station in life, and when I die he will be my heir."

His voice ceased and for a moment there was a

silence that seemed more impressive than words. Then Alister exclaimed:

"That is exceedingly generous of you, Sir. I am more grateful than I can possibly say."

"I do not mind telling you, my boy," The Mc-Craig replied, "that when I came South I was somewhat anxious as to what sort of wife you had chosen. However, although Katherine regrettably is connected with the stage, she is everything I would have wished for the wife of the future Chieftain of the Clan."

He looked at Shimona as he spoke.

"Thank . . . you," she murmured.

She wished she did not feel so guilty and that they had not been obliged to deceive this fine old gentleman. She thought also how horrifying it would be if he ever found out the deception that had been practised upon him.

Because she felt guilty Shimona moved forward impulsively and kissed The McCraig on the cheek.

"Thank you for making Alister happy," she said.

She knew The McCraig was pleased at her gesture. Then as if he suspected them of being overemotional he said almost harshly:

"I am now going to say good-bye, Katherine, as I shall not expect to see you in the morning."

Shimona looked surprised and he explained:

"I am leaving very early, as I have been invited to stay the first night of my journey North with the Earl of Glencairn near Leicester. He is an old friend of mine, and I have promised to be his guest."

He looked at the Duke as he said:

"I hope, Ravenstone, it will not be inconvenient for me to leave at seven o'clock?"

"It is not in the least inconvenient," the Duke replied. "But are you certain it will not be too long a day for you?"

"I am used to rising early," The McCraig replied, "and as I wish to dine with the Earl, the sooner I am on the road the better!"

He held out his hand to Shimona.

"Good-bye, my dear. I hope it will not be too long before I may entertain you at Craig Castle, and that many relatives of your husband may have the pleasure of meeting you."

"I shall look forward to it," Shimona answered as she curtseyed.

"I shall doubtless see you in the morning, Alister," The McCraig said to his great-nephew.

"Of course, Sir."

This time they all escorted The McCraig to the foot of the stairs. He walked up without the aid of the bannisters and Shimona thought it was easy to think of him as a King in the Highlands.

As soon as he was out of ear-shot Alister said:

"I must go back to Kitty. If I am to be back here by half after six tomorrow morning, the sooner I am asleep the better!"

The Duke did not reply and Shimona had the idea that he despised Alister for thinking it a hardship that he must rise early.

Although she felt that she also should say good-night she moved back towards the Salon and when the Duke followed her the door was shut behind them.

She walked to the fireplace and he moved slowly across the room towards her, looking as he did so at her face bent towards the flames and the light from them shining on her fair hair.

"It is entirely due to you," he said, "that the campaign to improve Alister's finances has been overwhelmingly successful!"

There was a note in his voice which did not make it sound as complimentary as the actual words.

"I feel . . . ashamed," Shimona murmured. "The McCraig is so magnificent and so honest and straightforward that I am sure it is wrong of us to deceive him."

"We have discussed this already," the Duke replied. "There was no other way that he could be persuaded to make Alister his heir."

"Do you think when the time . . . comes that Mr.

McCraig will make a good . . . Chieftain?" Shimona asked in a low voice.

"Does it really concern you one way or the other?" the Duke enquired.

Shimona was silent. Then she said:

"Perhaps it sounds impertinent, but because I have been involved I do mind. I would not want the members of the Clan to be disappointed or disillusioned."

"I have a feeling," the Duke said, "that Alister has learnt a lot from associating with you these last two days. He may in future insist on his wife behaving as she should do."

"A wise man once said that when a stone is thrown into a pond the disturbance from it goes on rippling out and one has no idea where the consequences will end," Shimona said in a low voice.

"That is true," the Duke replied. "But the consequences that you have evoked can only be good."

"How can you be sure of that?"

"I am sure because of your intrinsic goodness."

Shimona looked at the Duke in surprise.

Then as their eyes met she felt once again that strange magnetism that held her spellbound and made her feel almost as if he was drawing her towards him.

She made a little movement as if she would break the spell and the Duke said:

"I want to talk to you, Shimona. Sit down."

His voice was very serious. Her eyes widened and there was a questioning look in them before she obeyed him.

"First of all," he began, "I want to give you the money that was promised to you and which you have earned so brilliantly."

He took a sealed envelope from the table as he spoke and held it out to her.

Shimona took it automatically, but as she did so she wished she could refuse it.

Then she remembered that her father's life delaid it beside her on the sofa.

"I felt you would wish the money to be paid in pended upon it and with a little murmur of thanks she notes," the Duke said. "They are of a large denomination that can easily be changed."

Shimona did not speak and he went on:

"I would have preferred to pay it into a Bank for you. It could be dangerous for you to carry so much money about."

His words gave Shimona an idea.

"I have a message for Your Grace, from Mr. Bardsley."

"A message?" the Duke enquired.

"He asked," Shimona continued, "if you would pay the money you owe him directly into his Bank."

The Duke smiled.

"That is extremely sensible. If I gave Beau Bardsley notes, I am quite certain he would have given them all away long before he left the theatre. Have you any idea of the name of his Bank?"

"Yes . . . he told me it was Coutts."

"The money will be paid in tomorrow morning," the Duke said. "I gather you know Beau Bardsley well?"

"Yes."

"Have you asked his advice about going on the stage?"

"N-no."

"Then I am sure he would advise you against it as I do," the Duke said.

There was a pause before he went on:

"Tell me something, Shimona, and I want the truth. Have you as yet played a part in the theatre?"

She looked up at him and somehow it was impossible to lie.

"Not . . . yet."

"That is what I suspected," the Duke replied. "Now listen to me. Whatever you may feel about the glamour and lure of the theatre, you are wrong—completely and absolutely wrong!"

"Why should you say that?" Shimona asked.

"Because I know the theatrical world," the Duke answered, "and while some women, although very few, can reach the top of their profession simply through their talent, for the rest it is a very different story."

Shimona knew what he was trying to say, but because she was embarrassed she could only look into the fire.

"I do not believe for a moment," the Duke went on, "that you could cope with the sordid intrigue which is necessary for an actress to obtain a part she wants, or even to get a hearing, without someone to fight her battles for her. Do you understand?"

"Y-yes . . . I understand," Shimona said in a low voice.

"Then give up this absurd idea," the Duke insisted.

Shimona rose to her feet.

"I think, Your Grace, there is nothing to be gained by discussing it."

"I have not finished all I wish to say."

Shimona looked irresolute.

Because she could not give the Duke the answers he wanted, she wished to run away.

On the other hand, she did not want to leave him, knowing this was their last night together and after tomorrow she would never see him again.

"You will tell me nothing about yourself," he went on, "but I am sure that the reason you wish to go on the stage is because you need the money."

She knew that he was feeling for words before he went on:

"What I am about to suggest may sound strange, but I want to help. I want to do what is best for you."

"Please . . . Your Grace . . . do not say any more."

"I must," he answered. "I want to offer you, Shimona, enough money so that you can be independent."

Shimona drew in her breath and now she was looking at him.

"I swear to you," the Duke said, "that I will ask

nothing in return except what you wish to give me. There are no conditions attached to my offer—none whatsoever!"

He spoke impressively and even as the words of refusal came to Shimona's lips he said:

"I think you know there is a great deal more I could say to you—a great deal I want to say. But I promised Beau Bardsley when he sent you here that you would leave my house as pure as when you came into it."

Shimona's eyes flickered before his and the colour rose in her cheeks.

"I have kept my promise," the Duke said, "but you will never know how difficult it has been and how much I have wanted to make love to you, to tell you that you are the most beautiful person I have ever seen in my whole life!"

"It . . . it is . . . n-not . . . t-true," Shimona stammered a little incoherently.

"It is true, absolutely true!" the Duke said. "But I gave that promise and I will not break it. So there is only one thing I can ask you: when may I see you again?"

Shimona drew in her breath.

"Never! We shall never . . . meet again!"

"Do you really mean that?"

"It is . . . impossible . . . I cannot . . . explain . . . but it is impossible!"

"And you will not accept my offer of independence?"

Shimona shook her head.

"No, Your Grace. I know you mean it kindly, but you have given me everything I want."

"Five hundred guineas?" the Duke queried. "My dear child, how long do you think that will last?"

"Long enough," Shimona answered.

She was thinking that with the five hundred guineas her father was to receive they would be able to stay abroad for at least six months.

"Enough for what?" the Duke enquired.

Shimona did not reply and he exclaimed almost angrily:

"Why must you be so mysterious? Why must you perturb me by giving me no explanations—by leaving me knowing as little about you now as when you first came?"

She did not answer and he said:

"That is not quite true. I know a great deal about you—about your character, your personality, your sweetness, and indeed your purity."

He struck the mantelpiece with his clenched fist as he said:

"Knowing what I feel, do you really think you can walk out of my life and that after tomorrow I shall never see you again? It is impossible! Completely impossible!"

"It is . . . something you have to . . . accept."

Shimona paused before she added:

"If it makes you . . . happier, I will . . . not go on the . . . stage."

"Then what will you do? Where will you be?"

"I am going . . . abroad."

"Abroad?" the Duke echoed. "To live? And do you think that wise when there is also the possibility of war breaking out with France again?"

"Italy may not be involved," Shimona said quickly.

"So you intend to go to Italy."

She realised she had made a slip and therefore did not answer him.

"I have a feeling that if you reach Italy this year, you may not be able to return."

He came a little nearer to her.

"Who are you going with? Is it a man who is taking you away from your own country and everything that is familiar? Are you marrying him?"

Shimona gave a deep sigh.

"I cannot answer any of those questions, Your Grace. I think it would be wise now for me to retire to bed."

"I think it would be wise," the Duke replied, "but I do not intend to let you go until you tell me the truth."

"I cannot . . . please . . . I cannot!"

"I have asked you to trust me."

"I . . . I want to . . . but it is impossible . . . I swear to you that it is . . . impossible . . . otherwise I would do so."

She was pleading with him and he reached out his hand to take her chin in his fingers and turn her face up to his.

"Could anyone look like you," he asked almost savagely, "and yet be ready to deceive me?"

"I am not . . . deceiving you."

It was difficult to speak because the touch of his fingers gave her a strange sensation.

He did not release her but looked deeper into her eyes and seemed to come closer.

"You are so beautiful!" he said. "So unbelievably, incredibly beautiful!"

Because the note in his voice made her breathless and because her throat seemed somehow to be constricted, Shimona put up both her hands as if to ward him off.

"Please . . ." she begged, "please . . . you are frightening me."

The Duke took his fingers from her chin.

"I do not wish to do that, but you are driving me mad!"

There was a fire in his eyes which made her tremble but she managed to stammer:

"You . . . you will . . . forget me, and thank you . . . Your Grace . . . for all your . . . kindness."

"Do you really mean that?" the Duke asked. "What can I say? How can I persuade you that you must not go?"

"I have to," Shimona answered. "There is nothing . . . more to be said . . . and it will only make . . . everything more . . . complicated."

"Why? Why?" the Duke asked. "Why can you not tell me the truth? What are these secrets you are hiding?"

Shimona turned to pick up the envelope from the sofa.

"Good-night . . . Your Grace."

"If you really mean never to see me again," the Duke said, "and if you do intend to go abroad where I cannot find you, then will you let me kiss you good-bye?"

She did not answer and he said with a twist to his lips:

"It is not much to ask, and may I say it is something I cannot remember having asked before in the whole of my life."

He looked down at her worried little face and he said very softly:

"You do not have to tell me that you have never been kissed, and I want more than my hope of Heaven to be the first."

Shimona told herself she should not listen to him, that she should leave the room immediately.

She tried to think of her father, but somehow everything seemed to be swept away from her but the Duke's pleading voice and the strange feeling she always had when he was near to her.

She looked up at him and was lost.

There was something in his eyes that was irresistible, something too which seemed to unite them in a manner which Shimona could not explain, and yet was a wonder she had never known before.

He came closer still and now very gently, as if he was afraid to frighten her, he put his arms round her and drew her to him.

Vaguely, far away at the back of her mind, she thought she ought to struggle, but it was impossible.

There was a rightness, something inevitable about what was happening that might have been planned since the beginning of time.

"You are so perfect!" the Duke murmured, then his lips touched hers.

It was a kiss so gentle, so tender, that Shimona was not afraid and she was conscious of feeling secure and protected because the Duke's arms were round her.

Then as his mouth took possession of her she felt as if everything beautiful she had ever heard and seen was concentrated into a feeling that was an ecstasy of wonder and joy.

The room disappeared and there was no longer the warmth of the fire, the fragrance of the flowers, or the light from the candles.

There was only a sky brilliant with stars and they were alone beneath it, a man and a woman who had found each other across eternity.

The Duke drew her closer still and now his lips became more insistent and more demanding. At the same time, there was still a gentleness that precluded fear.

How long the kiss lasted Shimona had no idea.

She only knew when finally he raised his head that she felt dazed and bewildered as if she had fallen back to earth from the very heights of Heaven.

For one moment she looked up into his eyes.

Then with an inarticulate little murmur she turned and ran from the room, leaving him standing, staring at the closed door long after she had left.

* * *

Shimona had to wait for a long time on the doorstep before, after repeated rat-tats on the knocker, Nanna came to open it.

"My dearie!" she exclaimed when she saw who was standing there. "I'd no idea it'd be you, but you're so early. It's not yet six o'clock."

"I know," Shimona answered.

She walked into the house and the cabby who had brought her from Berkeley Square carried in her small trunk.

She paid him and when he had gone Nanna asked:

"What's happened? Why are you here at this hour?"

"It is all right," Shimona said soothingly. "I wanted to get away as soon as I could. I have the money,

Nanna. We can leave for Italy as soon as Papa is able to travel."

Nanna did not answer and Shimona said quickly:

"Why do you look like that? How is Papa?"

"I don't like the look of him," Nanna replied. "The Doctor came yesterday and he's coming again this morning, but I won't lie to you, dearie, he seems to be sinking."

"I will go to him."

Shimona pulled off her cape, flung it on a chair, and ran up the stairs.

Her father's room was in darkness.

She pulled open the curtains and let in the grey misty light of the early morning.

Now she could see him lying against his pillows and she knew that what Nanna had said was true.

There was something transparent about his face that had not been there before.

He had always been too thin, but now his cheeks were hollow, there were dark lines beneath his eyes, and there was altogether an insubstantial look about him.

Shimona stood looking at him for a long time. Then as he still seemed to be asleep, she made up the fire and went from the room.

Nanna was carrying her trunk upstairs.

"Has he been coughing very much?" Shimona asked.

"Sometimes in his sleep," Nanna answered, "and very badly when he is awake. The Doctor's kept him drowsy and he hasn't realised you've not been here."

"We must try and persuade him to take some food," Shimona said.

It was however difficult and although she tried to coax her father into eating a little breakfast he would only drink a cup of coffee and shook his head to every other suggestion.

"You must get strong and well, Papa."

"I am—tired," he replied in a far-away voice. "Too tired to—think, too tired to—act."

As if the word "act" impinged upon him he said in a different tone:

"Act! Are they—expecting me at the—theatre?"

"Not to-day, Papa," Shimona answered. "To-day is Sunday."

It was not true, but she thought it would prove as an excuse for him to rest and she gave a sigh of relief as his head went back against the pillows.

"What am I—playing on—Monday?" he asked after a moment.

"Hamet," Shimona replied. "You are playing Hamlet all next week and the theatre is sold out."

She felt sure that this was what he would want to hear.

There was a faint smile on his lips as Beau Bardsley said:

"That should mean—they will be able to—pay the staff."

"Yes, of course, Papa."

Nanna came in to tidy the room and when she had done so she said she would wash and shave the Master. She sent Shimona downstairs to prepare him an egg whipped up in milk.

"Add a little brandy to the glass," she said. "It'll give him strength if he won't eat anything."

When Shimona came upstairs again her father was coughing.

Perhaps it was because he had been moved while Nanna washed him, but whatever the reason he was coughing with a wrenching, rasping sound which seemed to shake his whole body.

He coughed and coughed, and now there was more blood on his handkerchief than there had ever been before and Shimona looked at Nanna with frightened eyes.

Finally Beau Bardsley lay back exhausted and Shimona was terrified by his pallor and by the difficulty he had in breathing.

It was then she heard a knock at the door and guessed that it was Dr. Lesley.

She sped down the stairs and when he saw her he exclaimed:

"I am glad you are back, my child! If you had not been I intended to send for you."

He saw the question in Shimona's eyes before he drew her into the small Sitting-Room.

He did not speak and after a moment Shimona said:

"I have the money. If Papa is well enough I can take him abroad."

Dr. Lesley was still for a moment before he said very quietly:

"I think, Shimona, you would rather know the truth. It will be impossible for your father to travel anywhere. In fact, my dear, there is nothing I can do to save him!"

* * *

Shimona used to wonder later how she would ever had managed without Dr. Lesley.

When her father died, he had done everything and in fact it was difficult for her to realise what was happening, except that she had an intolerable sense of loss.

She had somehow never imagined that he would die as her mother had, so quickly. One moment they were there and the next there was just an empty void which nothing could fill.

And yet his death had been beautiful, in a way he himself would have wished to die if he could have chosen it.

It was in the afternoon of the day that Shimona returned home. She was sitting alone by her father's bed-side, striving to face the truth of what Dr. Lesley had told her and trying vainly to believe that a miracle might still save her father.

The light from the fire cast a glow upon his face and he did not look so pale and insubstantial as he had done early in the morning.

With his clear-cut features and square forehead he looked like a Greek statue, and Shimona wondered if any man could be more handsome or more compelling than her father.

But even while she thought about him, it was impossible not to remember the attraction of the Duke and the irresistible expression in his eyes which had held her spellbound.

She had only to think of him to feel a quiver go through her and to know again that strange rapturous sensation that she had felt when he kissed her.

She did not for a moment regret that she had let him hold her in his arms and that for the first time in her life a man's mouth had possessed hers.

"I will always have that to remember," she told herself, "even though I shall never see him again."

Even if her father died and she did not go abroad, their paths would never cross.

The Duke lived in one world and she in another, and she had done the only thing possible in running away so that after the wonder and perfection of his kiss they had not descended to the bathos of commonplace words.

In letting him kiss her and hold her in his arms she had brought down the curtain on what she knew would always be the most wonderful experience in her life.

Sitting by her father's bed-side, she now admitted to herself that what she felt for the Duke was love, the same love that had made her mother run away from Bath, and from her rich and distinguished fiancé, with an actor.

But the love of Annabel Winslow, a Lady of Quality, for a distinguished young actor was different from the love of a daughter of an actor for a noble Duke.

Even if he wished it, which Shimona was sure he did not, they could never marry. It would be the same *mésalliance* that Alister McCraig had made in marrying Kitty Varden.

"I love him . . . but our love must never be spoilt or defamed," Shimona told herself.

Even in her innocence she knew that what he

felt for her was different from what he had felt for other women.

It was not the licentious, debauched Devil of whom her father had spoken who had offered her independence and promised at the same time that he would ask nothing in return.

She had known by the sincerity in his voice that he meant what he had said.

It might have been a difficult promise to keep. It might have proved quite impossible for them to be near each other and not succumb to the magnetism which drew them together.

But at least the offer had been made, although she thought no-one, certainly not her father, would have believed it.

"I believe the Duke," Shimona told herself, and felt an irrepressible yearning to see him again and talk to him.

Never had she thought anything could be so fascinating as to see him sitting at the head of his table, distinguished and at his ease, driving beside her in his Phaeton, or at that last inevitable moment when he had put his arms round her and drawn her close against him.

"I love him! I love him!" she whispered.

Then she felt ashamed that she should be thinking of the Duke when her father was near to death.

But love was something which no-one could control. Her mother had said once:

"When I first loved your father, I realised that nothing else was of consequence in the whole world —not my family, my friends, or the men who courted me. Everything seemed to vanish except for one man."

Shimona had not really understood at the time, but now she knew exactly what her mother had meant; for that is what had now happened to her.

It was what she had felt when the Duke kissed her and she was no longer in this world but in some enchanted place where they were alone, completely alone, save for the wonder of their love.

He had told her she was like a twinkling star, and she thought when he kissed her that the stars fell from the Heavens to lie at their feet.

"I love him! Oh, God, how much I love him!" she told herself, and knew that the future was dark and empty because it would not contain the Duke.

A coal fell in the fire and Shimona rose to pick it up with the tongs and put it back.

When she turned towards the bed she saw that her father's eyes were open.

"Annabel!"

She hardly heard the word, and yet it was spoken. She moved towards him.

"It is Shimona, Papa."

She put her hands on his and bent forward towards him, but he did not seem to see her.

"Annabel!" he said again. "Oh, Annabel—my darling!"

There was a sudden vibration in his voice, the same tone that vibrated through an audience and made them feel that everything he said touched their hearts.

Shimona felt the tears start in her eyes. Then still with that strange note thrilling through his voice, Beau Bardsley said:

"Annabel! It has been so long! My beloved, how I have missed you!"

It seemed to Shimona that for a moment there was a radiance in his face that seemed to transform him and a light in his eyes that was indescribable.

Then his eyes closed but there was a smile on his lips, and Shimona knew that he was dead.

* * *

It was Dr. Lesley who decided that for Shimona's sake the funeral should take place very quietly before it was announced to the public that Beau Bardsley was dead.

He arranged everything and the only mourners who followed the coffin to the graveside were herself and Nanna.

It was a wet, blustery day and Nanna sobbed as

the coffin was lowered into the grave and the earth thrown upon it, but Shimona was dry-eyed.

She knew that her father and mother were together again.

His body was enclosed in the plain oak coffin which Dr. Lesley had ordered, but his spirit was happy with the radiance which had been in his face and the joy that had vibrated in his voice.

"I am the one who has been left behind," Shimona told herself forlornly.

She had driven back from the funeral in a hired carriage, with Nanna still wiping the uncontrollable tears away from her eyes.

It was impossible for them to talk that day and Nanna shut herself in the kitchen, as she always did when she wished to be alone. Shimona went to her mother's Sitting-Room to look at the portrait of her father over the mantelpiece.

She found it hard to realise that never again would she hear him come back to the house in the evening to tell her what had happened at the theatre or lie in the bed upstairs learning his lines for his next performance.

She knew that she had to plan what she and Nanna would do in the future.

Thanks to the Duke's concern for his nephew, they had enough money for it not to be an urgent matter. At the same time, she knew it would not last forever.

It was impossible for Shimona not to keep thinking of the Duke, remembering everything he said to her, going over and over again the moments when they had been together.

Sometimes she wondered whether she would have been happier if she had never gone to Ravenstone House. If she had not tried to earn the money which was to save her father's life, she would have saved herself from having a broken heart.

That was what she had.

She had always laughed at the phrase when she had heard it spoken in one of the plays.

Now she knew it could be a reality; for the pain

in her own heart seemed to grow day by day, and she was never free of it.

However much she tried to tell herself sternly that it was a thing of the past and something to be forgotten, she longed for the Duke with an intensity which at times frightened her.

And almost insidiously the temptation came to her to do as he wished, to accept his terms, to tell him that after all she would agree to anything he suggested as long as she could sometimes see him.

Then she told herself that that was only the first step to destruction.

She was not so foolish nor so ignorant as not to be aware that the reason why her father did not wish her to be associated with the theatre was the loose morals which seemed inevitably involved in theatrical life.

It had been impossible for Shimona not to understand when it was said that the leading lady was under the protection of some nobleman who had financed the production, or that the producer had pushed his current mistress into an important part simply because he found her attractive.

Even though her father was careful about what he said in front of her, the gossip of the theatre was part of his life.

Shimona was astute enough to piece disjointed sentences together and know the truth, even when her father and mother attempted to hide it from her.

It did not really shock her; she only thought that it was unpleasant or, as Dr. Lesley had said, "unsavory," and she knew that as far as she was concerned such a life would be entirely and absolutely wrong and contrary to everything in which she believed.

'The love that Papa and Mama had for each other,' she thought, 'was a very beautiful, holy thing.'

She was sure, although she had never come in contact with it, that illicit love was the opposite.

And yet it was hard to believe that her love for the Duke and his feelings for her were anything but right and good.

There had been something unmistakably spiritual in the feelings he had evoked in her.

She had felt when he took her up towards the stars that they were both a part of the Divine, and her love was in fact as holy as her prayers and the feelings of reverence she had in Church.

"How can that be wrong?" she asked.

But she knew the answer. There was nothing wrong in what she had done so far, but she must go no further.

"What will become of us?" she asked Nanna two days after her father's funeral.

"I've been thinking about that," Nanna replied. "We've got to face facts, Miss Shimona. We can't live here forever!"

"Papa owned the house."

"Yes, I know," Nanna agreed, "but there's rates to be paid, repairs to be done, and we have to eat."

Shimona looked at her wide-eyed as she went on:

"I've been thinking that if I went out to work we could perhaps keep going for at least a year or so."

"Do you really think I would sit here and let you work for me?" Shimona asked. "That is absurd, Nanna. If anyone works it should be me. I am young and strong."

"And as innocent as a new-born babe!" Nanna finished scornfully. "What do you think you could do?"

"I do not know," Shimona answered. "There must be something."

She gave a little sigh.

"Perhaps after all I could go on the stage."

"And have your father and mother turn in their graves?" Nanna asked furiously. "That's the last thing you'll do, Miss Shimona, and then over my dead body!"

"Well, what else is there?"

"We'll think of something."

Shimona knew they were the consoling words of a Nurse to a fretful child and that, despite the effort she made to deceive her, Nanna was really worried.

"Well, I've not got time to think about it now,"

Nanna went on in a brusque tone. "I want to get down
to the shops. We're out of bread and I want to buy
some eggs for supper. At least we've enough money
not to starve for the next month or two."

"Shall I come with you?" Shimona asked.

Nanna looked towards the window.

"It's drizzling," she said. "You've been out once
today. You keep by the fire and put the kettle on in
about half an hour. If I see a muffin-man, I'll buy some
muffins for tea."

"That will be nice," Shimona smiled.

She knew Nanna was trying to give her a treat.
She had always loved muffins when she was a small
girl and would listen for the muffin-man's bell as he
came down the street carrying the tray on top of his
head.

Nanna bustled away with an empty basket on her
arm and Shimona sat down in front of the fire.

She wondered what the Duke was doing now.

Perhaps, she thought a little forlornly, he was
with a beautiful woman, elegant and sophisticated,
someone who amused him and talked the language of
the world in which he lived.

They would have private jokes about the people
they both knew. They would gossip about the famous
personages she had read about in the newspapers.

Perhaps he would be going to dinner at Carlton
House to be surrounded by more beauties like the
Duchess of Devonshire, Lady Jersey, and the fascinating Mrs. Fitzherbert, who had captivated the Prince
for so many years.

'I am not part of the social world, I am not part
of the theatrical world, I do not belong either in the
city or in the country. In fact I belong nowhere!'
Shimona thought dismally. 'I am just an "odd one
out." '

It seemed strange that when the day before yesterday the newspapers had been full of reports of
Beau Bardsley's death there was no mention of her.

They had all of them revived the story of how her

father had run away from Bath with the beautiful
Annabel Winslow.

But apparently they had forgotten, if they had
ever known, that the handsome actor and the beautiful
Society girl had produced a child.

Dr. Lesley had brought Shimona all the newspapers so that she could read the glowing obituaries
that had been written about her father.

There had been a long column in the *Times*
and another in the *Post* besides a news report about
the financial state of Drury Lane now that the actor
who had brought in the audiences was no longer there.

One correspondent had written:

"Something will have to be done, but it appears that no-one in the management has any
idea what it should be."

There were many sketches in the newspapers
of Beau Bardsley in his leading roles, but even when
she had read everything that was written about him
Shimona felt that there was so much left un-
said.

The newspapers did not describe his generosity
and his kindness to his fellow-actors, and none of them
had understood how his whole life had centred round
his home, his wife, and daughter.

"I have protected you from the newspapers as I
know your father would have wished me to do," Dr.
Lesley said.

But because she was so anonymous to the extent
that no-one had ever heard of her, Shimona could not
help feeling that she had died too.

The house which had once held three happy
people united by their love for one another was
now only a hollow shell.

Sitting in front of the fire, she was just thinking
that it was about time she put the kettle on when she
heard a knock on the front door.

She thought perhaps Nanna had forgotten her

key, and jumping to her feet she ran across the small hall and opened the door.

Then she gave a gasp, for it was not Nanna who stood there in her black cloak and bonnet, but the Duke.

He was even more resplendent than she remembered, with his starched white cravat, the points of his collar high above his chin, and his high hat at an angle on his dark head.

As they stared at each other, it seemed to Shimona as if she had flown across the world to find the person who was waiting for her on the other side of it, and she felt an extraordinary sense of homecoming, security, and protection.

"Shimona!" the Duke exclaimed.

She thought that her name had never sounded so attractive as it did spoken in his deep voice. Then slowly, as if he forced himself to remember his manners, he took his hat from his head.

"May I come in?" he asked. "There is a great deal I have to say to you."

She opened the door a little wider and he walked into the hall and seemed much too large for it.

Shimona shut the door behind him and without speaking led the way into the small Sitting-Room.

The Duke looked up at Beau Bardsley's portrait over the mantelpiece.

"Now I understand! You are Beau Bardsley's daughter, but I had no idea he had one!"

"Papa would never . . . allow me to have . . . anything to do with the . . . theatre," Shimona answered, wondering why her voice sounded so strange.

"I can understand that," the Duke said, "and yet he let you come to me to act the part I required."

"Papa was . . . unconscious and knew nothing about it. I came because I needed the money to take him abroad. I hoped it would . . . save his life."

There was a perceptible quiver in her voice and the Duke said:

"I asked you to trust me."

"I dared not do so," Shimona replied. "Papa

would have been so . . . angry that I did not . . . intend to tell him anything about it . . . until he was well."

"I understand," the Duke said. "Shall we sit down? I have a lot to say to you, Shimona."

"Yes . . . of course," Shimona answered. "I apologise, Your Grace, for my bad manners. I was not expecting to see you."

"I know that," he answered. "How could you have done anything so cruel as to slip away from the house before anyone was awake? When they told me you had left I could hardly believe it!"

Shimona said nothing, and seeing the colour come into her cheeks and the flicker of her eyes he knew what she was thinking.

"I was determined to find you again," he said after a moment. "I went to the theatre to be told that Beau Bardsley was away ill. I thought it was only a temporary indisposition. I called the next day and the next, until I saw the newspapers and learnt he was dead."

"How did you manage to find this house?" Shimona enquired.

The Duke smiled.

"I was not going to be defeated," he answered, "and I remembered that you had asked me to pay the money I owed Beau Bardsley into Coutts Bank. They gave me his address."

"I never thought of that."

"I thought you could not have," the Duke replied, "and now I have found you, I will not allow you to hide from me again."

She did not answer and after a moment he said in a gentler tone:

"I am very sorry about your father. He will be deeply missed, as you well know. No-one could act as he could, or look so compellingly handsome."

His eyes went up to the portrait as he added:

"I can see now a faint resemblance between you. If I had had any sense I would have noticed it before."

He looked round the room.

"So this is the private part of Beau Bardsley's

life upon which no-one was allowed to encroach. Having seen you, I am not surprised that he was so protective. He was right in trying to keep you safe."

Shimona sat down in a chair opposite him, her fingers locked together, and the Duke knew she was very tense.

"I would not do anything to distress you," he said quietly, "but once again, Shimona, I need your help."

"My help?" she questioned.

"I suppose we might have expected that our little charade could not really have such a conclusive and happy ending."

"Something has gone ... wrong?"

"Not exactly wrong," the Duke answered, "but The McCraig, having reached safely the home of the Earl of Glencairn near Leicester has been taken ill."

"Oh, no!" Shimona replied. "I am sorry."

"I understand it is not a dangerous illness," the Duke said, "and I think myself it is just exhaustion. For a man of eighty to travel so many miles must have taken its toll of his strength."

"Yes ... of course," Shimona murmured.

"The McCraig has, however, decided that before he returns to Scotland he will set his house in order. In other words, he will settle on Alister the sum of money he promised and will also make a new will. But before he does so, he wishes to see you both."

Shimona stiffened.

"To see ... me?"

"It is quite understandable," the Duke smiled. "After all, a great deal of money is involved and I think he wishes to impress upon Alister exactly how it should be expended."

"But . . . why should he want . . . me to be present?" Shimona asked.

"That of course is entirely your fault," the Duke said with a smile. "You have captivated him, Shimona. He was delighted with you, and if he wants to see you again then who shall blame him? I am in exactly the same boat!"

Shimona looked away towards the fire.

"It is impossible!" she said after a moment.

"Why?" the Duke enquired.

She tried to find a reason but there did not seem to be a very valid one.

There was no longer her father to be kept in ignorance of her movements. There was in fact no-one.

Yet underneath the apprehension she felt at committing herself to acting a part and again deceiving The McCraig, there was an irresistible excitement because she would be able to go on seeing the Duke, at least for a little while.

"When I found you," the Duke went on, "hoping that perhaps someone in Beau Bardsley's household would have some idea of where you might be, I was going to suggest that you and I could drive to Leicester together and Alister could follow in his own Phaeton."

Shimona did not reply and he went on in a beguiling tone:

"Of course if you prefer to go in a closed carriage I shall understand, but personally that is something I abominate on such a long journey."

"Yes . . . of course . . . I should like to . . . drive with you," Shimona said in a small voice, "but . . ."

"What is worrying you?" the Duke asked.

"I do not know," Shimona replied. "It seems . . . wrong somehow to . . . go on with this . . . pretence."

"When I was small," the Duke said, "my Nurse used to say that one lie always leads to another."

Shimona smiled.

"I am sure your Nurse said the same thing," the Duke remarked.

"She often says it," Shimona replied. "But The McCraig is such a kind old man."

"He can be a hard, tough one, when it suits him," the Duke said. "He has needed a great deal of persuading before he could see that as the next Chief, Alister was entitled to some consideration."

He paused before he said quietly:

"I am quite certain that, if you had not been you, he would not have been half so generous."

Shimona gave a little sigh.

"I wish you would tell him the truth."

"That is completely and absolutely impossible," the Duke said firmly. "He would feel defrauded and insulted, both of which are intolerable to a Scotsman!"

Shimona was silent for a moment. Then she said:

"Could you not do . . . without me?"

"I think it would be impossible," the Duke replied. "Will you tell me why you are so reluctant to do what I ask of you? Can it possibly be that you do not trust me to behave as you would wish me to?"

He saw the colour come into Shimona's cheeks and he added quickly:

"I promised your father that I would do nothing to hurt you, and I swear that the last thing I would want to do now would be to shock or frighten you."

He paused for a moment before he added very softly:

"Do you believe me?"

"I believe you!" Shimona answered.

"Then what worries you?" the Duke asked. "If you are not afraid of me, why are you afraid?"

"I . . . think of . . . myself," Shimona said in a low voice. "I thought I would . . . never see you again . . . I told myself I had to . . . forget everything that had . . . happened . . . and now you are here."

"Did you really think I would let you go?" the Duke asked. "I had every intention, Shimona, of seeing you again and finding you however cleverly you hid yourself away."

"But . . . but . . . why?"

"Because something happened between us that was different from anything that ever happened to me before," he answered. "Even now I cannot explain what you mean to me. I just know that I cannot lose you."

He gave a sigh before he said:

"It is like finding an incredible treasure. You know it is one, and yet there is so much you have to learn about it before you are aware not only of its true value, but also of its history and its very existence."

He bent towards her.

"That is what I feel about you, Shimona. You are unique! Someone who seems to have come to me from another world."

He was speaking with a note of sincerity and also passion in his voice. Then as their eyes met it seemed as if the words they were saying to each other were quite unnecessary.

"That . . . is what I . . . feel too," Shimona whispered.

"My precious! My darling!" the Duke exclaimed.

He put out his hands towards her as the door opened and Nanna came into the room.

Chapter Five

Driving away from London, Shimona thought it was incredible that she should really be with the Duke and that they were journeying towards Leicestershire.

The whole entourage was an excitement she had never known before.

First she was travelling with the Duke in his yellow and black Phaeton with a groom up behind wearing the Ravenstone livery, as were the four outriders with their white wigs and black velvet peaked caps.

Alister followed them in his own Phaeton, although his team of four horses was not of such magnificent horse-flesh as the Duke's.

Behind them again came the Duke's travelling-chariot with Nanna, very straight-backed and disapproving, sitting inside.

It was Nanna who nearly made it impossible for Shimona to undertake the journey.

When she had returned to the house to stand in the Sitting-Room, her face rigid with disapproval, the Duke had risen to his feet.

"I will leave you now," he said to Shimona. "I have to tell Alister I have found you and make arrangements for tomorrow. I will return later this afternoon to tell you what is planned."

When he had gone Shimona faced a storm of protest.

She had hoped before she went to Ravenstone House that Nanna had never even heard of the Duke.

But her very first words as the door closed behind him told Shimona all too clearly that she had not only heard of him but also knew a great deal about him.

"What's that wicked man doing here?" she enquired angrily. "He wouldn't have dared to cross the threshold when your father was alive."

"He is the Duke of Ravenstone, Nanna," Shimona answered.

"I know well enough who he is," Nanna said. "His groom told me whose Phaeton was waiting outside our door. You're not to speak to him again! D'you hear me, Miss Shimona? You're not to have anything to do with him."

"That is impossible, Nanna."

"Why should it be impossible?" Nanna enquired.

Hesitatingly, because Shimona was choosing her words with care, she told Nanna that it was the Duke who had paid her five hundred guineas for pretending to be his nephew's wife and it was his money that had been paid into Beau Bardsley's account in Coutts Bank.

"You'll send it back immediately!" Nanna said. "His money's tainted and no decent person would lay a finger on it!"

"It will not be very decent for us if we starve!" Shimona answered.

"You can't touch pitch without being contaminated," Nanna retorted. "I couldn't eat a mouthful if I thought it was paid for by a Duke who is a disgrace to his name and his family!"

Shimona did not speak and she went on:

"I've heard your father often enough saying he's known in the theatrical profession as 'His Disgrace' and that's what he is—not a fit person for you to know about, let alone speak to."

"It is too late for all that now," Shimona said wearily. "I know him, Nanna, and I must help him."

"Over my dead body!" Nanna said firmly.

"His Grace has always been polite and considerate towards me."

"And what was he saying as I came into the room?" Nanna demanded. "He was speaking to you as no gentleman worthy of the name should speak to a lady who is unchaperoned, a girl who has no more idea of the wickedness of the world than a newly born kitten."

Nanna ranted on and on, until finally she said:

"You're not going to Leicester with the Duke and that's that! What you're going to do is meet your grandparents."

"My grandparents?" Shimona exclaimed in surprise.

"I've been thinking it over," Nanna said, "and there's nothing for it but for you to go where you belong."

"Do you mean Mama's parents, or Papa's?"

"I believe Canon Bardsley is dead," Nanna replied, "but about two years ago your mother's father, Sir Harvey Winslow, was still alive. I saw his name in one of the newspapers."

"But he said he would never speak to Mama again, after she ran away with Papa. She told me so."

"Hot words are often spoken in anger," Nanna answered, "and unless Her Ladyship has changed a great deal in the years, she always loved her daughter and she'll love you."

"If they did not wish to know Mama, then they will have no wish to know me."

"They may not even know of your existence, and when they do, I'm as certain as I stand here that they will welcome a grandchild."

"It is no use talking about it, Nanna! I am not crawling to them on my knees!"

"I'm going to get in touch with them," Nanna said, "and nothing you can do or say'll stop me. I know it's the right thing. Anything would be better than being mixed up with that evil man and his goings-on."

"What has the Duke done that has upset you so much?" Shimona asked.

"I've been hearing bad things about him for years," Nanna answered. "I've heard your father denouncing him over and over again, and he and your mother told me of the way in which he behaved to that poor Miss Minnie Graham."

"That was a girl who was acting with Papa," Shimona said almost beneath her breath.

"Pretty little thing she was, but she was led astray like so many others and then there was no saving her."

"What happened to . . . her?" Shimona asked in a low voice.

"When the Duke was tired of her she found another gentleman to expend his money on her," Nanna answered scornfully. "Playing the lead, she was, at Birmingham when your father last spoke of her."

She gave a kind of snort which was a regular sound of hers when she was disgusted.

"The wages of sin are not always death in this evil world," she remarked tartly.

"Whatever the Duke has done or not done in the past," Shimona said, "I have to go with him tomorrow. I cannot let him down and I cannot ruin Mr. McCraig's life or upset his Great-Uncle."

"You've no call to be getting into such a tangle, Miss Shimona," Nanna cried angrily. "Never have I heard of such a mess, and what your mother would say I don't know!"

"I have to go, Nanna."

"I'll speak to His Grace when he returns," Nanna said grimly, and that was all Shimona could get out of her.

But the Duke had his way.

Nanna asked him into the Dining-Room and they were in there a long time while Shimona waited in the Sitting-Room feeling apprehensive of the outcome.

What would the Duke think of being talked to severely by a servant?

If he was offended by it, he might walk out of the house without saying good-bye to her.

She felt she was being torn in pieces by the conflict that was taking place.

She could understand only too well what Nanna felt, and she knew that the condemnation in her voice was exactly the same as there had been in her father's when he spoke of the Duke.

But how could she make anyone understand how differently he had behaved to her?

How there existed something between them that seemed to contradict his reputation and the scathing manner in which people denounced him.

Then she told herself that perhaps she was being deceived.

What did she know about men—or any man—and especially anyone who was as important as the Duke?

Was there perhaps one law for the aristocrats and one for ordinary people? And had her father been more censorious than someone else might have been simply because of his upbringing?

It was so difficult for her to know the truth, difficult to be fair. She had to admit that the Duke must have behaved disgracefully in some ways, otherwise his reputation would not have reached the ears of her mother and herself.

But whatever he had done, Shimona felt she was in honour bound to finish what the Duke had called their "charade" in which she had taken a part to help Alister McCraig.

If he was exposed now, if his Great-Uncle realised that he was married to the sort of actress that he had supposed, then everything would be much worse than if he had told the truth from the very beginning.

"I am committed! I must help him!" Shimona told herself, and wondered how much longer the Duke and Nanna would be in the Dining-Room.

At last the door of the Sitting-Room opened and he came in.

Shimona realised that he did not shut the door behind him and that Nanna was waiting in the hall.

"Everything is arranged," he said, "and there is only one change in our plans."

"What is that?" Shimona asked nervously.

"As I do not exactly see eye to eye with the Earl of Glencairn, I have sent a groom to Leicester to ask The McCraig if he will honour me by being my guest at my own house. It is not far from where he is staying, not more than five miles, and I think it would be more comfortable for all of us if there were no strangers present."

"I can understand that," Shimona said, remembering that she must pretend to be Alister's wife.

"Then everything is arranged," the Duke said, "and I will call for you at half after nine, if you can be ready."

"I will be ready," Shimona promised, her eyes alight with relief because Nanna had not been able to prevent her from going with the Duke.

There had been no chance of a private conversation between them, and only now when they were alone in the Phaeton did she ask:

"You are not . . . angry?"

"Angry?" he enquired. "Why should you expect me to be?"

"I thought perhaps Nanna was rude to you yesterday and you might be . . . incensed about it."

The Duke smiled.

"She was not rude," he answered. "She was only very firm, as Nurses always are. I rather felt I was back in the Nursery and being punished for some extremely reprehensible misdemeanour."

"I was afraid of that," Shimona said in a low voice.

"It was what I deserved," the Duke said, "and you should not have taken part in what your Nurse described as 'disgraceful goings-on.'"

Shimona laughed because she could not help it.

"Nanna was very shocked. She has never allowed me to lie."

"And quite rightly so."

He was keeping something back from her, Shimona thought, and she looked at him a little apprehensively.

She felt as if some barrier had been erected between them, but she was not certain what it was and anyway it was impossible to put her feelings into words.

The Duke was charming, polite, and somehow reserved, but when they had luncheon together in a private parlour at the Coaching-Inn he looked at her with an expression in his eyes which made her feel shy.

Alister had gone ahead to meet a friend at Northampton and Shimona had been half afraid that Nanna
would insist on being with her. But without any argument Nanna and the valet lunched in the Travel-
lers' Dining-Room.

They had driven very swiftly for a great number
of miles and Shimona was hungry.

It also seemed for the first time since her father
had died that the misery that had encompassed her
like a fog was lifting and she was once again in the
sunshine.

She had thought never again to see the Duke,
and yet she was now with him. She was hearing his
voice, he was near her, and because he was there her
sensation of wonder and joy was increasing every moment.

She had taken off her travelling-cloak with its fur-
lined hood which had framed her face, and while they
had their meal her hair was very fair against the dark
oak panelling of the Inn.

When they finished and the servants left the room
her eyes were very blue as she lifted them to the
Duke's face.

"I . . . thought I would . . . never see you again,"
she said in a low voice.

"That was your decision—not mine."

"I knew how . . . angry Papa would be, but it was
the only way that I could have taken him to . . . Italy."

She thought the Duke would want to talk to her
about it and perhaps tell her again that he had minded
the thought of losing her, but to her surprise he rose
from the table to say:

"If you have finished, I think we should be on our
way."

There was somehow a harsh note in his voice
and something she did not understand in the way he
looked away from her, his eyes seeming to avoid her
face.

"What is . . . wrong?" she asked.

"Why should you think that anything is wrong?"
he queried.

"Something has changed you. It must have been something Nanna said. Please . . . please do not listen to her. I have never . . . believed the things that she has been . . . told about you."

"You have—never—believed them?" the Duke repeated slowly. "What have you been told about me?"

Shimona made a little helpless gesture with her hands.

"Nothing very positive. Just that Papa did not approve of some of the things . . . you have . . . done."

The Duke walked towards the log-fire to stand with his back to Shimona, looking down into it.

"Your father was perfectly right," he said, "and I am sure everything you heard about me was the truth. Come, we still have a long way to go before it gets dark."

There was nothing Shimona could do but put on her cloak and follow him outside to where the Phaetons were waiting.

There were fresh teams of horses belonging to the Duke to convey them, which she learnt were always kept ready on the road to Leicester in case at any time the Duke should require them.

Nanna was also waiting to see her into the Phaeton.

"If it gets cold or begins to rain, Miss Shimona," she said, "you're to travel with me. I've no wish for you to get a chill."

"I am very warm, thank you, Nanna," Shimona replied, "and the Phaeton has a hood that can be raised if we require it."

Nanna pursed her lips together and Shimona hurried away so that she could not argue any more.

She wished in some ways that Nanna had not come with her, but she knew she must have insisted on it to the Duke; and he in fact would think it only correct that a lady should travel with her lady's-maid.

'But I am not a lady,' Shimona thought miserably. 'I am only the daughter of an actor, acting a part, and more unhappy than I have ever been in my whole life because I am in love.'

She was unhappy at the moment because the Duke was unpredictable and because she was becoming more and more convinced that a barrier had been erected between them.

Yet he had only to smile at her or to speak to her in that deep voice for her heart to turn over in her breast and for her to feel as if the larks were singing in the sky above them.

"I love him!" Shimona told herself as they journeyed on.

She thrilled every time her shoulder touched his arm and every time he turned his head to look at her and their eyes met.

It seemed then as if it did not matter what he said or how he behaved.

The feeling they had for each other was still there, and while he might exert a rigid control on every other part of him he could not control the expression in his eyes.

"How long are we going to stay at your house?" Shimona enquired.

She tried to speak normally and not to allow her anxiety to reveal itself in the tone in which she spoke.

"I have an idea that The McCraig will not wish to linger once he has made his will," the Duke said. "He is an old man and he wants to be with his Clan as much as possible before he dies."

"He is really ill?" Shimona enquired.

"No, I think it was just an indisposition caused by too much travelling," the Duke replied, "but it has certainly been to Alister's advantage."

"When will Mr. McCraig join us again?" Shimona asked.

"He said he would pick us up the other side of Northampton," the Duke replied.

Sure enough, in another few miles they saw Alister McCraig in his Phaeton waiting for them at a crossroads.

They did not slacken speed but waved and he fell into line behind them.

"Do you always travel in such grandeur?" Shimona asked, looking at the outriders and thinking how smart and impressive they looked.

"I like to be safe from highwaymen and I like my comfort," the Duke replied. "If we were to break down and were forced to stay in some uncomfortable Inn, one of my servants is an excellent cook, and they can all look after me as well as my valet does."

"I suppose that is what one would expect of a Duke," Shimona replied, thinking a little wistfully how they had never been able to employ more than one maid to help Nanna in the house.

"There is no particular virtue in comfort," the Duke said, "but it is something which, like money, makes life very much easier. Thanks to you, Alister will now live in a comfort he never expected."

"It is nice that you should be so concerned about him."

"You must not find virtues in me which I do not possess," the Duke replied. "It is my fault entirely in the first place that Alister was in danger of losing his inheritance."

"How could that be true?"

"I introduced him to Kitty Varden!"

"But you did not expect him to marry her?"

"Good Heavens—no!"

There was silence. Then in a very low voice Shimona said:

"Did you think he might . . . wish her to be his . . . mistress?"

For a moment there was another silence, until the Duke said angrily:

"Will you not talk in such a manner? It does not become you and there is no reason for you even to know of such things!"

Shimona looked at him in surprise and he went on:

"Your Nurse is right. What you are doing now can only have a corrupting influence, and the sooner it is all over the better!"

His mouth was set in a hard line when he finished

speaking, and he used his whip for almost the first time since they had left London, as if he wished to hurry his horses on to their destination.

Shimona relapsed into silence. There seemed to her nothing she could say.

She only felt inexpressibly that she was alone.

They reached the Duke's house, which was called Melton Paddocks, as the afternoon was drawing to a close.

As they came down a straight drive it stood in front of them and was not, Shimona thought, a particularly attractive house.

The centre block was three storeys high with two wings of only two storeys reaching out on each side like two arms.

She thought they must have been a later addition to a Queen Anne building and she was to learn later that she was right.

She had the impression that the house did not welcome them, but it was quickly dispelled as the Phaeton was drawn to a standstill and servants in the Duke's livery came hurrying from the front door and she saw The McCraig waiting to greet them.

"I hope you have not been here long, Sir," the Duke said as he held out his hand to the old gentleman.

"No, indeed, I arrived only half an hour ago," The McCraig replied.

They went into a large room which was, Shimona thought, extremely masculine in the manner in which it was furnished.

There was a long leather sofa and arm-chairs and the walls were decorated with paintings of horses and dogs.

"I am glad to see you, my dear," The McCraig said to Shimona.

"I am sorry you have been ill, Sir."

"Not ill," he said sharply as if he resented the thought of a weakness. "Just a trifle tired and a little troubled with my heart."

"Your heart?" Shimona asked quickly.

"A passing twinge," The McCraig said lightly. "But I wanted to see you and Alister before I went North."

"And I am very pleased to see you again," Shimona smiled.

He patted her shoulder affectionately. Then she was introduced to the Duke's agent, a Mr. Reynolds, who was in charge of the house and the Estate.

"I hope everything will be to Your Grace's satisfaction," Shimona heard him say. "We did not have much time to prepare for your visit."

"I have told you before, Reynolds," the Duke said sharply, "that I do not intend to give long notice, or indeed any notice, when I wish to stay in my own house."

A Housekeeper was waiting to take Shimona upstairs, an elderly grey-haired woman in rustling black, and when she had shown Shimona into her bedroom she found Nanna there.

"You are not too tired, Nanna, after such a long journey?"

"I've been worrying about you, sitting in an open carriage when you should have been inside with me in the warm."

"I am warm enough," Shimona answered, "and I like being in the fresh air."

But Nanna did not wish to talk.

She made Shimona lie down before dinner, and because she was in fact more tired than she would have admitted she fell asleep.

When she awoke it was to find that her clothes had been unpacked and there was a bath waiting for her, with one of her prettiest gowns laid out on the bed.

"I hope you had someone to help you, Nanna," she said, realising how much had been done while she was asleep.

"There's been help of a sort." Nanna sniffed disdainfully. "But this is not a happy house, Miss Shimona. I know that already."

"How can you be sure?"

"A bad master makes a bad servant!" Nanna snapped.

Shimona gave a little sigh. She felt she could not bear another argument over the Duke at this moment, and she was well aware that Nanna had come North determined to find fault with everything.

"I expect the servants resent us turning up at a moment's notice," she said. "You know yourself how difficult it is to have everything prepared so quickly."

"The Housekeeper's too old for her job, if you ask me!" Nanna snapped.

She went on grumbling all the time Shimona was having her bath and getting dressed. But as she went downstairs she was too happy at the thought of seeing the Duke and being close to him to worry about Nanna or anyone else.

She had hoped to have a chance of talking to him alone before they were joined by the others, but Alister McCraig was already in the Sitting-Room with the Duke and The McCraig joined them a few seconds later.

"I have arranged for Glencairn's Attorney to attend us after dinner, Ravenstone," he said. "I hope that will not be inconvenient?"

"No, of course not, Sir," the Duke replied.

"I sent him a draft of my intentions this morning, which I asked him to translate into legal language. All I will have to do is to sign the documents. It would be a help if you would witness my signature."

"I am at your service," the Duke replied.

The McCraig looked at Shimona.

"I think, my dear," he said, "you will be pleased with my arrangements!"

"I am sure I shall," Shimona answered.

"I am leaving to you personally my wife's jewellery," The McCraig went on. "I think you will find the sapphires, which are unique, will become you, but then so will all the jewels."

"B-but . . . please . . . I cannot . . ." Shimona began frantically, then she saw the Duke frown and the words died away on her lips.

She knew The McCraig would think it very strange if she refused to accept the gift he offered her.

Then she thought quickly that of course the jewellery would be bequeathed in the name of Katherine McCraig, Alister's real wife.

"It is very . . . kind of you, Sir," she managed to stammer to The McCraig.

"I can think of no-one I would rather have own it than yourself."

Shimona drew in her breath.

The pretence and deception were far harder to bear than she had anticipated and she was thankful when they could move into the Dining-Room where the conversation in front of the servants was of other things.

The Attorney, who looked exactly like a caricature of his profession, Shimona thought, arrived with his black bag containing the documents and a number of large white quill pens with which they could be signed.

They sat round a table in what Shimona learnt was the Breakfast-Room, and the Attorney read aloud in a dry, crisp voice the long legal document which he had prepared on The McCraig's instructions.

Although he was very long-winded about it, the disposition of the money was quite clear and straightforward.

Alister McCraig was to receive £100,000 for his immediate use and he was, on his Great-Uncle's death, to inherit his entire fortune and any personal effects that were not already entailed onto the Chieftain.

The value of the whole amounted to a very large sum, and Shimona thought that, after he had heard the contents of the Will, Alister McCraig seemed to walk taller and to have a pride and a presence that had not been there before.

She remembered how the Duke had said that Alister's father had quarrelled with The McCraig and she thought that it was unfair that he should have suffered through a disagreement that was not of his making.

It had not only left him poor, but maybe with a sense of inferiority.

Perhaps it was for that reason that he had married Kitty Varden, she thought perceptively, as an act of defiance because he wished to assert himself.

She was sure, despite the fact that he was somewhat insignificant, that Alister McCraig was at heart a nice human being.

The Attorney's voice seemed still to rasp in their ears after he had left.

The Duke had insisted on them all drinking a glass of champagne to celebrate what he said was a special occasion, and they wished The McCraig a safe journey home.

"I am going to insist that you both come to see me in the spring," The McCraig said to Shimona and Alister. "If it had been possible I would have liked to take you back with me now."

Alister parted his lips to protest, but The McCraig went on:

"I know you will have many other commitments. But next spring I shall not take no for an answer."

"It is something we will both look forward to," Alister said.

"And so shall I," The McCraig replied with his eyes on Shimona.

She smiled at him, hoping that she would not have to lie again, feeling that every word of deception she uttered seemed to stick in her throat.

It was still early but The McCraig wished to retire to bed, and although Shimona hoped there would be some excuse for her to talk to the Duke alone they all moved in a body across the Hall and seemed to expect her to follow The McCraig up the staircase.

It may have been her imagination, but Shimona fancied that the Duke did not look at her as he bowed in return to her curtsey.

She went to her bed-room, where Nanna was waiting.

"You should not have waited up, Nanna," she exclaimed. "You must be tired and as you well know I am quite capable of putting myself to bed."

"If other servants don't know the right way to behave—I do!" Nanna answered.

"What has upset you now?"

"I told you this is a bad house, and that's what it is!" Nanna retorted. "The men-servants were drinking too much below stairs—disgusting I call it!—and the maid-servants from all I hear are no better than they ought to be!"

"What do you mean by that?"

"It's not something I should be repeating to you, Miss Shimona, but you might as well know what sort of place you are in."

Shimona was well aware that this was all a thinly disguised attack upon the Duke, and because she was quite certain that Nanna would have her say whatever she replied she asked a little wearily:

"What has happened?"

"I can hardly believe it, Miss Shimona," Nanna replied, "but on the floor above us there is at this moment a baby that had no right to be born into the world."

"A baby?" Shimona enquired. "How do you know?"

"The Head Housemaid told me about it," Nanna said. "Not that she knows her place. She wouldn't be accepted in any Household I've worked in."

"What did she tell you?" Shimona asked.

"That one of the kitchen-maids, little more than a child, she is, gave birth to a baby three days ago."

"Here in the house?"

"Upstairs, as I've just said."

"Do they know who the father is?"

Shimona was almost afraid of the answer.

"Apparently one of the grooms," Nanna replied. "A married man, with a wife and three children, so he's not prepared to stand by her."

"Poor girl!" Shimona murmured.

"Poor girl indeed!" Nanna exclaimed. "And what

do you expect with such an example from those who should know better?"

Shimona did not need to ask what Nanna meant, knowing she was determined to have her say.

"There's parties that take place in this house, Miss Shimona, when the Duke comes here for the hunting, that I would not soil your ears by repeating. I was told about them downstairs, and they were enough to make any decent person's hair stand up on end!"

"I do not think it is any of our business, Nanna."

"I should hope not!" Nanna retorted. "As I've already said, Miss Shimona, a bad master means bad servants, for there's always fools ready to follow those who set a bad example."

There was no use in arguing, Shimona thought.

When at last Nanna had left her, still muttering to herself, and she was alone, she could not help feeling sorry for the girl upstairs who had given birth to an illegitimate baby.

Had she perhaps been wildly in love with the man to whom she had given herself? Had she thought that nothing mattered save the feelings they had for each other?

And if she was young, had she been aware of what the probable consequences of such an action might be?

She remembered how she had said to the Duke that the circles from a stone thrown into a pond will cast ripples outwards indefinitely.

Was it really the example of the Duke that had caused his kitchen-maid to produce an illegitimate child?

How could they have known when they tried to save Alister McCraig from the consequences of an uncomfortable marriage that she would be left all the jewellery that had belonged to The McCraig's wife?

One thing led to another and it was so easy for people to be hurt or even destroyed by a wrong action.

Shimona remembered that she had not said her prayers and because she was still unhappy about the strange barrier between her and the Duke she prayed that he might find happiness.

"Make him happy, God," she prayed. "Let him clear himself of all that is wrong and wicked, and please, whatever sins he has committed, do not let there be any ill consequences from them."

She prayed for him from the very depths of her soul, thinking that one unavoidable consequence was that she loved him.

For good or bad, whatever happened in the future, she would love him and go on loving him all her life.

It was a love, she was sure with an inescapable conviction, which would defy time and she would never be free of it.

She had known that even when she thought she would never see the Duke again, and now she had snatched one more day with him.

He had said when he came to her home that he would never let her go, but she had the uncomfortable feeling he had changed his mind.

It was nothing he had put into words, she just knew it instinctively, as she knew that her whole being reached out towards him.

She longed for him and for the closeness they had known when he had held her in his arms in Ravenstone House.

There they had been one and Shimona thought despairingly that perhaps never again would she know the rapture and wonder of feeling that they were part of the Divine which he had given her.

"I love him!" she whispered into her pillow.

Then irresistibly and unmistakably she knew what she wanted and although she knew it was something she should not say she prayed aloud:

"Oh, God, make him love me enough to want to ... marry me!"

* * *

It had been a tiring day and Shimona drifted away into a dreamless slumber.

She awoke suddenly to feel as if she was still travelling, the wheels still rumbling beneath her, and there was the soft sway of the Phaeton, the jingle of the harness.

Then she opened her eyes and remembered where she was.

The fire had died down but the coals were still glowing and she could see the outline of the bed against them.

Everything seemed very quiet, but she felt as if something had disturbed her.

"I am being imaginative," she told herself, and yet she found herself listening.

What she expected to hear she had no idea, she just listened.

She could hear nothing but the sound of her own heart.

'I must go to sleep,' she thought.

Even if The McCraig left for Scotland tomorrow, the Duke had promised at dinner that he would take her and Alister to see his horses, which meant they would not return to London until the following day.

Shimona felt her heart leap at the thought. She would be able to talk to him. There was so much she wanted to know, so much she wanted to learn from him.

She could ride well. Her mother had insisted upon that, because she herself had always been an extremely good rider.

When they could afford it they had hired the best horses from a livery-stable and either rode in the Parks or even sometimes ventured outside the city into the open countryside.

Shimona thought she would like the Duke to see her on a horse, for she was sure he would admire a woman who rode well.

But never in her wildest dreams had she imagined she would be able to ride anything so superlative as the horses which the Duke owned.

"Do you own race horses?" she had asked him at dinner.

"I have some in training," he replied, "but I really prefer steeple-chasing when I can ride my own animals. I like to do things for myself, not watch other people doing them for me."

Alister had laughed.

"Is that why I never see you at a Mill, Uncle Yvell? I believe in fact you are a rather good pugilist."

"I box sometimes at Gentleman Jackson's Rooms," the Duke answered.

"And you fence also," Alister said. "If you are not careful, they will call you a Corinthian."

"They have many other more appropriate titles for me," the Duke said cynically.

As if he thought it would be a mistake for The McCraig to know too much about the Duke's reputation, Alister changed the subject.

But Shimona had heard the bitterness in the Duke's voice, and because she loved him she wanted to say something which would make him smile and forget his unpleasant thoughts, whatever they were.

"How can he be all the things they say he is?" she asked herself now. "I do not believe it. I do not believe what anyone says."

She felt she wanted to proclaim her faith in him to the world. She wanted to defend the Duke against his enemies. She wanted to hold him in her arms and protect him as if he were a child who was being bullied.

'I suppose that is love,' she thought. 'Love that makes me want not only the ecstasy of his loving me, but also to mother him, to look after him and save him from anything that could hurt him.'

She lay in the darkness feeling that her thoughts and prayers were winging their way towards him. Then as she lay there she was aware of something strange.

If was not what she heard, although she felt it was that for which she had been listening, but something she smelt.

She lay for some moments to make sure that she was not mistaken, then she knew that it was smoke.

She got out of bed and reached for her winter dressing-gown which Nanna had laid over a chair by the bed.

It was made of turquoise-blue velvet and warmly lined with thick satin. Shimona put it on and slipped her feet into little boots of silver lamé lined with fur which she always wore when it was cold.

She buttoned her dressing-gown high at the neck and down the front and as she did so she pulled the bell sharply two or three times.

It must be late, she thought, but the bell would ring upstairs, and one of the house-maids would hear it.

Whether they did or not, she must arouse everyone for now the smell of smoke was stronger than it had been before.

Even as she turned towards the door Shimona heard a bell begin to ring, and the cry, far away, but coming nearer: "Fire! Fire! Fire!"

Chapter Six

As Shimona reached the door it was flung open and the Duke stood there.

He saw Shimona and said quite calmly:

"The house is on fire. Go downstairs and out into the garden."

He did not wait for her answer but turned to run along the passage, and she knew that he was going to warn The McCraig.

She noticed that he was still wearing his evening-clothes and knew it could not be as late as she had thought, as he had obviously not yet gone to bed.

She moved out onto the landing and looking over the bannisters saw a turmoil in the Hall where men were moving pictures and furniture out of the Sitting-Rooms.

Alister, also in his evening-clothes, was directing them through the open front door.

Shimona was just about to descend the staircase when there was the sound of panic-stricken voices, women were screaming, and down the stairs from the top floor came a number of servants.

The women, who had obviously been aroused from bed, wore shawls or blankets over their night-gowns and they were being propelled down the stairs by the men who were still in their livery.

"Come on! Get on with you! You've got to get out of here!" one of the men was saying roughly.

Shimona remembered what Nanna had said and thought he was the worse for drink.

She stood to one side to let them rush down the stairs. Then she saw that one woman was being

carried by a footman and as she passed Shimona
heard her cry weakly:

"My—baby! My—baby!"

No-one appeared to hear or to take any notice,
but all down the staircase Shimona could hear her
crying even above the noise and commotion which
the others were making.

"They have left the baby behind," she told herself.

The smoke was not yet very thick although it
was beginning to sting her eyes. She looked up the
staircase and saw that it was clear and the fire,
wherever it was, was not on the top floor of the
building.

Impulsively, without thinking it might be dangerous, she ran up the stairs to see if she could find the
baby who had been left behind.

Before she reached the top landing she heard it
crying, and as there was an oil-lamp outside the bed-
room it was not difficult to locate which one contained
the child.

She found it lying on the bed and she knew the
servants in their haste to get the mother to safety
had overlooked the fact that the baby was lying beside her.

It was a very small baby and for its size it
seemed to make quite an inordinate amount of noise.

It was wrapped in a shawl and Shimona pulled
a blanket from the bed and wrapped it in that too.
Then she started back down the stairs.

She could not move very quickly because she
was not only hampered by the child in her arms but
also by the fact that her velvet dressing-gown reached
to the floor and she was unable to lift it.

When she reached the lower landing the smoke
had become much thicker, and when she tried to
move through it she saw that the staircase down to
the Hall was now in flames.

For the first time Shimona realised the danger
she was in.

Now she hurried away along the passage, feeling

there must be another staircase which would take her down to the ground floor.

The smoke seemed to grow thicker and thicker. She groped her way through it and felt cold air on her cheeks.

A moment later the smoke cleared and she saw in front of her a long window which was open.

'I must have missed the staircase,' she thought.

Looking through the window, she saw that it led out onto a flat roof and realised that the window opened out from the main building onto one of the side wings which she had noticed when she first arrived.

It seemed to be the obvious thing to go out onto the roof rather than brave the thick smoke which had obscured the staircase she was trying to find.

She had to stoop to get through the window and did so with care so as not to hurt the baby.

It had ceased crying and was only whimpering as if it was hungry.

It was easy to walk on the roof and Shimona moved towards the parapet, realising that the light which made it easy for her to see her way came from the fire in the downstairs rooms of the main part of the house.

The flames were crackling ominously even as she reached the parapet, which was about a foot high.

She looked down into the garden below and saw the household congregated on the lawn.

They also saw her, because although Shimona could not hear what they said she could hear their raised voices and she saw several hands pointing in her direction.

The flames were hot and she moved further along the building until she reached the end of it.

"Now that they have seen me," she told herself, "it should be easy for someone to find a long ladder so that I can climb down into the garden."

She turned and gave a frightened gasp as she realised what a hold the flames had by now on the house.

From where she was standing she could see them belching out like crimson tongues from the lower windows and the smoke was rising in a black cloud high above the roof.

"It is a good thing I saved the baby," she told herself. "It would have had no chance of surviving."

She looked down below and saw through the smoke there were men running in the garden towards where she was standing and she thought she could discern a ladder in their hands.

Then to her consternation she was aware that the flames were not only widespread in the main part of the house, but were also now appearing at the side of the wing on which she was standing.

'This wing also must have caught fire,' she thought, and felt fear beginning to flicker inside her almost like the tongues of fire which were consuming the house.

Again she looked over the edge of the parapet.

The smoke made it difficult to see what was happening, but as yet there was no sign of any rescue party.

She looked back again towards the flames, then with a leap of her heart she saw a figure coming towards her from the open window and knew who it was.

The Duke came to her side and she saw that his white cravat was singed and there were dirty marks on his face.

"Why did you not do as I told you . . ." he began, then he saw the baby in her arms.

"They . . . forgot the . . . baby," Shimona answered automatically.

But her heart was singing with happiness because he had come for her and she was no longer afraid.

He looked down into her eyes, then he put his arms round her and held her as close to him as he could without hurting the baby in her arms.

"How could you do anything so absurdly brave?" he asked. "I heard a woman crying about losing her baby, but I did not realise that it was in the house."

"It is . . . quite safe," Shimona said a little incoherently.

It was difficult to speak because the Duke's arms
and the closeness of him made her feel that nothing
else was of any importance except the fact that they
were together again and there was no longer a barrier
between them.

She felt the Duke's lips on her forehead, then he
went to the side of the balustrade to shout:

"Hurry up with that ladder!"

As he spoke Shimona saw the tongues of fire rising above the parapet only a few yards from them.

The Duke must have seen it too, for he turned
back and began to take off his evening-coat.

"It is not going to be easy," he said, "because you
have to hold the baby, but I want you to do exactly
as I tell you to do and not be afraid."

"You are with . . . me," she whispered, "that is all
that . . . matters."

He had taken off his coat and now he made her
put her arms into the sleeves and because she was
so small they covered her hands. Then he pulled the
rest of the coat high up over her shoulders so that it
covered her head.

He covered the baby's face with the blanket and
said:

"Keep your head down and on no account look
up. Just trust me to guide you."

As he spoke he pulled her backwards to the edge
of the parapet, then he lifted her in his arms and
stepped onto the ladder.

He was holding Shimona close against him so
that he covered her back; one arm encircled her waist,
the other held on to the side of the ladder. Her head
was bent until she could see nothing and was in complete darkness.

They went down very slowly and now Shimona
could hear the roar of the flames, the crash of falling
masonry, and she knew that if the Duke had not been
holding her she would have been desperately afraid.

Step by step, step by step, they went lower and

lower, until suddenly the Duke released her, other arms took hold of her, and someone lifted the baby from her arms.

She tried to pull back the coat from over her face but she was being carried away from the noise of the fire and when finally she managed to see what was happening she was blinded by the glare of it.

The flames, now out of control, were leaping higher and higher and she saw the ladder on which they must have descended collapse at the same time as the roof of the building fell in.

She saw Alister's face through the smoke and realised that he had carried her away.

"The . . . Duke . . ." she murmured. "Where . . . is . . . the Duke?"

"He will be all right," Alister replied. "I am going to carry you to a place where you will be out of danger."

"The Duke . . . must have . . . been . . . burnt!" Shimona insisted.

"They are improvising a stretcher for him," Alister answered. "He will be following us."

Shimona tried to content herself with this information but, as Alister carried her across the garden and a little way down the drive, she could think of nothing but the flames leaping over the falling ladder.

She knew that as the Duke had guided her down, having given her his coat, he had protected her with his own body.

Alister carried her in through an open door and set her down on the floor in a small front room which was neatly furnished.

"This is your first guest, Mrs. Saunders," he said to a middle-aged woman who was arrayed in a red flannel dressing-gown.

"I'll look after her, Mr. McCraig," the woman replied.

"They are bringing His Grace here as well, Mrs. Saunders. I am afraid he has been burnt in the fire, and he will need the use of your best bed-room."

"It's all ready, Sir," Mrs. Saunders answered. "My

husband was certain you'd wish to use the house as soon as we heard the fire had broken out."

"A lot of people will have to be accommodated," Alister said, "but if you will look after His Grace and this lady, then that is all I will ask of you."

"I'll do my best, you knows that, Sir," Mrs. Saunders answered.

Alister turned to Shimona.

"You are all right?"

"I am all right," she replied. "Please . . . find out . . . what has happened to the Duke."

Even as she spoke she heard the sound of men's feet and a moment later she saw four men carrying a narrow gate on which they had laid the Duke.

Shimona looked at him and gave a cry of sheer horror.

He was lying face downwards and his back was bare while only the tattered remnants of his fine lawn shirt remained on his wrists and round his neck. The whole of his back had been burnt raw.

"Take His Grace upstairs!" Alister commanded.

With great difficulty the men negotiated the narrow stairway up to the landing while Mrs. Saunders had gone ahead to open the door of the front room.

"We need a Doctor," Shimona said.

"I know that," Alister answered, "but he lives at least six miles away, and I am told he will not come out at night."

Shimona for the first time felt panic-stricken.

She did not need to be told how seriously injured the Duke was. Then to her relief she saw Nanna coming through the doorway.

She put out both her hands towards her.

"Oh, Nanna. His Grace is terribly burnt. What can we do about it?"

It was a child crying for help and Nanna automatically responded.

"We'll look after him, Miss Shimona. Don't you worry."

Then she went up the stairs, and Shimona followed her.

As she reached the top she heard Alister say: "I will be back later."

Then he was gone and a moment later the men who had carried the Duke upstairs passed her on the small landing and also left the house.

The Duke was lying on his face in the centre of a big double bed which seemed almost to fill the room.

Mrs. Saunders was staring at his back.

In the light from the candles she had lit it was even more horrifying than it had seemed in the dim light downstairs.

"It'll kill His Grace," she said after a moment. "There's naught they can do for burns as bad as those!"

"Something has to be done!" Shimona answered fiercely. Then she gave a sudden cry. "Nanna, do you remember when you scalded your foot what Mama used to heal it?"

"Honey," Nanna replied. "But that was a small burn, nothing like this!"

"Mama always said that honey should be used on burns—and all wounds!" Shimona said. "And it will stop the pain."

"That's true," Nanna agreed, "the pain will be unbearable if His Grace recovers consciousness."

"If . . . ?" Shimona whispered beneath her breath.

Then she said to Mrs. Saunders:

"Have you any honey in the house?"

"Indeed I have, Miss. We keeps our own bees and my larder's full to bursting with the good crop we had this summer."

"Then please fetch it up here."

"And bring us some of your old sheets," Nanna added. "I'm sure anything we destroy His Grace will replace."

"I'm not worried about that," Mrs. Saunders answered. "You're very welcome to all I have."

The two women left the bed-room and Shimona stood looking down at the Duke's body.

It seemed impossible that any man could be so badly burnt and be still alive, and she knew that the pain he had endured as he carried her to safety protecting her with his own body must have been intolerable.

"How could he have done that for . . . me?" she asked herself, and felt the tears gather in her eyes.

She brushed them away and for the next hour she worked with Nanna to cover the whole of the Duke's body with a thick layer of honey.

They poured it over his raw skinless back, then they bandaged him with the sheets which Mrs. Saunders tore into strips.

They had also to bandage his arms and the backs of his legs where his silk stockings had been burnt away to leave nothing but singed flesh.

Only his face and his hands were unmarked as they discovered when they turned him over, and his thick satin evening-breeches had protected him from waist to knee.

"He gave me . . . his coat," Shimona said miserably after they had been working for some time.

"I know, dearie, I saw what he did," Nanna answered. "He's a good man, whatever they may say about him."

When the Duke was bandaged so that he looked like a cocoon, Nanna sent Shimona from the room while she and Mrs. Saunders cut his breeches away and put him between the sheets.

It was only then that Shimona felt the reaction of what she had passed through sweep over her like a tidal wave.

When Nanna came to find her she was sitting on the floor of the landing outside the Duke's room, fast asleep.

Shimona did not even stir when she was put to bed in a small room at the back of the house.

She did not wake until Nanna came to call her in the morning, looking her usual self in one of her own dresses, which had somehow miraculously been saved from the fire.

The moment she was awake Shimona sat up in bed to ask:

"His Grace? How is he?"

"He has not regained consciousness," Nanna answered. "And as Mr. Alister tells us they are expecting the Doctor sometime this morning, I thought you would wish to get up and tell him that we can nurse him and need no interference."

If Shimona had not been so worried she would have smiled.

She knew that Nanna disliked all Doctors with the exception of Dr. Lesley and had complete faith in the potions that her mother had prepared over the years.

She realised too that if Nanna had taken the Duke under her wing she would not have to fight to stay and look after him as she intended to do.

There was however one urgent question that mattered more than anything else.

"He will . . . live, Nanna?" she asked. "We will be able to . . . save him?"

"With God's help we will," Nanna replied.

* * *

The following days seemed to pass almost in a dream.

It was difficult for Shimona to think of anything or even to remember to eat and drink in her anxiety about the Duke.

When finally he regained consciousness, Nanna gave him one of the herbal draughts she had prepared and he went to sleep again.

"The longer he's not aware of what's happened, the better!" she said when Shimona questioned her. "I'm doing what your mother would have done, and that'll prove to be right."

Shimona was sure this was true, but it was difficult not to be desperately anxious and she found it hard to think of anything but the man she loved—the man who had saved her life.

Ten days after the fire had taken place, Alister asked to see her and she left the Duke's bedside to go down to the small front room where he was waiting.

He had called every day, having accepted the responsibility that the situation demanded, to find out how the Duke was, and she learnt that he had been very busy taking charge of everything in his Uncle's absence.

He was being, Shimona thought, surprisingly efficient; in fact he seemed a different person.

She had heard from Nanna after the first night that everyone had been housed in the farm cottages, and that quite a number of the valuable pictures and pieces of furniture in the house had been saved.

Even her own gowns which had been shut in a heavy wardrobe had only been slightly scorched and were in fact wearable.

But most of the rooms in the main part of the house had been damaged and the wing from which she had been rescued had been completely gutted.

The fire had started, Shimona learnt, because one of the men-servants who had drunk more than the rest had overturned an oil-lamp.

None of the others had been in a fit state to put out the fire until it was out of control.

"Mr. McCraig's sacked the agent—and not before time," Nanna told her.

"Sacked Mr. Reynolds?" Shimona questioned.

"It was his fault in letting the Household staff get out of hand."

Three days after the fire Shimona had learnt that Captain Graham had come from London to supervise everything.

The Duke's valet, Harris, who was housed in a nearby cottage, was always there if they needed him, and Captain Graham made no changes where their lodging was concerned except to improve the menu.

Luxuries appeared which were well beyond the cooking capabilities of Mrs. Saunders.

The outrider whom the Duke had spoken of as being an excellent cook was now in charge of the small kitchen.

The Chef, like most of the other servants who

had been at Melton Paddocks, had been dismissed.

"A clean sweep was what was wanted," Nanna said with satisfaction.

Alister was waiting for Shimona when she went into the Sitting-Room and she saw by the expression on his face that he had something grave to impart.

"What is it?" she asked apprehensively.

"I know you will be sorry, Shimona," he replied, "but my Great-Uncle died last night."

"Oh, no!" Shimona exclaimed in consternation.

"As you know, he had a slight heart-attack after we got him away from the fire," Alister explained. "He seemed to get better and talked of going North in a day or so. But last night he must have had another attack and when his valet called him this morning he was dead."

"I am sorry . . . so very sorry."

"So am I," Alister said in all sincerity.

He hesitated for a moment, then he said:

"You will understand that I have to take his body North. He would not wish to be buried anywhere except among our own people."

"Of course," Shimona murmured.

"I will leave Captain Graham in charge," Alister went on, "but there is something I want to ask you."

"What is it?" Shimona asked.

Alister seemed to feel for words and then he said abruptly:

"When this is all over—will you marry me, Shimona?"

Shimona stared at him in astonishment, thinking she could not have heard him correctly.

"M-marry you?" she replied. "But I thought . . ."

"So did I," he answered. "I knew that Kitty had been married before, but she told me that her husband had died in prison. It was not true."

Shimona found it difficult to say anything and he went on:

"When he read what had happened in the newspapers and it was reported that I was the heir to The McCraig, the man came to see me and asked for

twenty thousand guineas to disappear and not to
make any furture claims upon his wife."

"What . . . did you . . . answer him?" Shimona
managed to say.

"I told him I would settle twenty thousand
guineas on Kitty, who could then resume their rela-
tionship if she wished to do so."

"So you are . . . free."

"I am free," he said. "But I know that my Great-
Uncle was right when he said you were exactly the
right sort of wife for the Chieftain of the Clan Mc-
Craig."

He paused before he added a little self-con-
sciously:

"I have also fallen in love with you."

"I am very honoured that your Great-Uncle
should have said such kind things about me," Shimona
said softly, "and that you should think the same. But
I know you will understand when I say that I could
not marry any man I did not . . . love."

"And if I wait, so that we get to know each other
better, have I a chance?"

"I am . . . afraid . . . not!"

"You love someone else?"

There was silence and then Alister said in a
low voice:

"It is—Uncle Yvell, is it not?"

"Y-yes."

"Oh, my dear, he will break your heart," he
pleaded, "and I could not bear to think of that happening to you."

"There is . . . nothing I can . . . do about it,"
Shimona murmured.

Alister came to her side to take her hand in his
and raise it to his lips.

"You have taught me so much," he said. "If I
make something of my life in the future, if I become
in any way worthy to follow in my Great-Uncle's footsteps, then it will be entirely due to you."

"Thank . . . you," Shimona said.

Then he kissed her hand and left her.

When he had gone she went upstairs to the Duke's bed-room and sat down by his bedside.

He was asleep but he was looking better.

The pallor that had been there at first had gone from his face and he looked extremely handsome. She could only think, as she had thought again and again, how much she loved him.

She told herself that he must love her a little.

What man would have suffered as he had for her sake unless he had been activated by love?

And yet she was not certain.

It was somehow ironic that Alister should have asked her to marry him, when all she prayed for in her heart, even though she told herself it was impossible, was to hear those words from the Duke.

Nanna had come into the room without Shimona being aware of it.

Now she started as she felt her come up behind her.

"Don't look so worried, dearie," Nanna said in a low voice. "I've looked at the back of one of His Grace's arms this morning when we were making the bed. There's a new skin forming. Skin as clear and as flawless as that of a new-born babe."

"Oh, Nanna, is that true?"

"Would I tell you a lie?" Nanna enquired. "The honey has worked as your mother always said it would."

"I can hardly . . . believe it!"

"Oh, 'thou of little faith'!" Nanna said almost scornfully.

But Shimona wanted to go down on her knees and send a prayer of thankfulness and gratitude up to the sky.

* * *

The Duke grew better day by day and now it seemed to Shimona that she never had a moment to herself.

She read to him, she wrote letters and memoranda at his dictation. Although she had the feeling that

Captain Graham would have done it better than she did, the Duke wished to have her by him.

She even thought that when she was reading the newspapers or a book to him he was watching her face rather than attending to what she was saying.

Once or twice when she asked him a question about what she had read he certainly found it hard to give the right answer.

He did not talk very much and they had no intimate conversation—certainly nothing that could not have been said with a dozen people in the room.

But Shimona went to sleep with his name on her lips and awoke thinking of him.

When she was not with him, she felt part of herself was missing.

"I love him; I love him . . . there is nothing else in the world but him!" she would whisper over and over again.

The Duke slept in the afternoon and then both he and Nanna insisted that Shimona go out for a walk.

Her steps nearly always took her to the stables where Saunders or one of the other grooms would be waiting with a basket of apples cut into small pieces with which she could feed the horses.

Their heads would be over the lower door of their stables and they would reach out greedily for the pieces of apple she gave them in the palm of her hand.

Saunders would talk to her about the horses.

But it was Harris who told her the things she wanted to hear about the Duke.

She soon learnt that the valet had what was almost an adoration for his master, whom he had looked after, he told Shimona proudly, ever since he was a young man.

"Them as says things about His Grace don't know him as I do, Ma'am, and that's the truth!" he said.

He saw that Shimona was interested and he went on:

"His Grace has often warned me against speaking

of his private affairs, but I don't mind telling you, Ma'am, that he's done more good in his time than a great many other gentlemen in his position, and there's as many people living secretly on his bounty as there are on his official pay-roll."

This was the sort of praise that Shimona wanted to hear, and she only hoped that Harris said such nice things about the Duke to Nanna.

In fact, since the Duke had saved her from the fire Nanna had completely reversed her opinion of him.

"He saved your life, Miss Shimona," she said more than once. "If it hadn't been for His Grace, you'd have been burnt to a cinder. That roof collapsed a few seconds after you reached the ground!"

There were tears behind the words and then as if she thought she was being too sentimental Nanna would add almost angrily:

"Why you couldn't have done as you were told, Miss Shimona, and gone straight downstairs I don't know. I saw you on the landing and thought you were just behind me, but all that shoving and pushing by those hysterical women stopped me from getting to you."

"I had to save the baby, Nanna, you know that."

Captain Graham told her what had happened to it.

"The mother's more grateful than she can ever say. She wanted to come and thank you personally, but I thought you'd enough to put up with already."

"What has happened to her?" Shimona asked.

"I took her back to her parents. They're decent, respectable folk and they've taken her in. She's a pretty girl and doubtless she'll find someone who'll marry her."

"Oh, I do hope so! Perhaps . . . it would be . . . possible . . ." Shimona began a little hesitatingly, wondering how much money she could afford to offer.

"There is no need for you to worry about that," Captain Graham said. "I knew what His Grace would

want and I have provided her with what you might
call a handsome pension."

He smiled and added:

"The other servants who have been dismissed
have also been given a considerable sum of money to
tide them over until they can find other employment. I
have no doubt they will behave better in the future
than they have here."

Shimona on her walk looked at the house with
its burnt-out windows and wondered if the Duke
would rebuild it.

She still did not like to bother him with funda-
mental questions until he was better in health.

It was now well into November and she thought
that if he were leading an ordinary life the Duke
might be staying at Melton Paddocks for the hunting.

She wondered if the reports of the parties he had
given had been exaggerated, or if in fact they had
been the orgies which Nanna had heard described.

"What happens at an orgy?" she wondered.

What did people do when they behaved in a
reprehensible manner which made other people like
her father not only denounce them but also speak of
what occurred with almost bated breath?

She felt very young and ignorant as she turned
away from the house, feeling despairingly that it was
ridiculous to think that the Duke might be genuinely
interested in her.

What had he in common with a girl who had
seen nothing of life, who might have been shut up in
a Convent for all she knew of the world and the sort
of entertainments that amused him?

She walked back towards the groom's house and
as the pale winter sunshine sank behind a distant
wood she forgot for a moment her sense of unhappi-
ness because of the beauty of the leafless branches
and boughs of the trees, silhouetted against the pink
and gold of the sky.

There was a touch of frost in the air and Shimona
thought that it would freeze during the night. Then

her footsteps quickened because it was time for her to
go back and she would see the Duke again.

"If for nothing else," she told herself, "I shall always bless the fire because I have had this time with
him . . . time when we have been together and even
when he was unconscious I was able to be near him,
to look at him."

She opened the door and the warmth of the small
house came towards her like a wave of welcome.

She pushed back her fur-trimmed cloak from her
face, unclasped it at the neck, and laid it down on a
chair.

She was just about to go upstairs when she realised that the door of the front room was open.

She could see the bright light of the fire and she
realised that someone was sitting beside it.

For a moment she could not believe it possible,
then as she went to the doorway she saw that sitting
in one of the big leather arm-chairs which had been
salvaged from the fire was the Duke.

He was dressed and his high, intricately tied cravat was very white against his face, which was much
thinner since he had been ill.

He looked amazingly handsome and very like
his old self.

"You are . . . up!" Shimona gasped.

"It was to be a surprise," he answered. "Forgive
me for not rising."

"No, no, of course, you must take things easily."

Now she ran across the room towards him, her
eyes wide and shining in her small face, her lips
parted with excitement.

"You are . . . not in . . . pain? You feel all . . .
right?" she asked almost incoherently, the questions
tumbling over each other.

"I am almost as good as new!"

Shimona laughed from sheer happiness. Then she
sank down on the woolly hearth-rug at his feet.

"I am so glad, so very, very glad! I was . . . afraid
when you were carried in here that you . . . would not
. . . live."

"I realise it is entirely due to you that my skin has healed and without a scar on it," the Duke said. "Your Nurse told me it was you who thought of using honey."

"You saved my life," Shimona said softly.

Her eyes looked up into his, but he turned his head to stare at the fire.

"Now that I am better, Shimona," he said in what she thought was a hard voice, "we have to make plans for your future."

Shimona was suddenly still.

"M-must we . . . talk about it . . . now?"

"We must," the Duke answered gravely. "Now that I am no longer an invalid you cannot stay with me unchaperoned."

Shimona looked at him in consternation.

She had forgotten, even if she had thought of it, that a chaperon where they were concerned was necessary.

"There are," the Duke went on after a moment, "two alternatives for you to consider."

Shimona looked at him in perplexity and he went on:

"The first is that you should go to your grand-parents, and this, before we came North, I promised your Nurse I would help you to do."

"I . . . thought Nanna must have said something like that to you," Shimona answered. "But I have already told her that I have no intention of getting in touch with relatives when for years they ignored my mother's very existence."

"A little while ago there was no alternative," the Duke said, "and I agree entirely with your Nurse that it was the sensible and practical thing to do."

Shimona did not speak and he did not look at her as he went on:

"Since we have been here I understand that you have had the opportunity of accepting a different position."

For a moment Shimona did not understand, then the blood rose in her cheeks as she said:

"Do . . . do you mean what . . . Alister suggested?"

"Alister wrote me a letter before he left and I read it when I was well enough to do so. He is very anxious that you should be his wife."

Shimona drew in her breath.

"I am . . . honoured that he should . . . wish it . . . but I cannot marry him."

"Why not?"

"I am . . . not in . . . love with . . . him."

"Is that really so important? You would have a great position in Scotland, and Alister speaks about you with a warmth of feeling of which I did not know he was capable."

"He was . . . very happy with the woman he thought he had married . . . or so he said . . . until he found that she already had a . . . husband."

"He thought he was happy," the Duke corrected, "but The McCraig and you made him see there were greater possibilities in himself than he had ever dreamt of."

He paused before he went on:

"I believe that when he gets older and is living amongst his own people, Alister will develop both character and personality."

"I think that too," Shimona agreed, "and I hope one day he will find a woman who will love him for himself and whom he will love with all his . . . heart."

There was an unmistakable little throb in her voice and after a moment the Duke said:

"So you have decided to go to your grandparents."

"There is a . . . third alternative," Shimona said in a very low voice.

He looked at her enquiringly and although she was shy she forced herself to meet his eyes as she said:

"You . . . offered me one . . . once."

"I offered you money and you refused it."

"If I . . . accept it now . . . would I be able to . . . see you . . . sometimes?"

She knew that he went rigid, then he said:

"That would be impossible and so I must withdraw my offer."

"Why . . . must you?"

She raised herself onto her knees and came nearer to his chair so that she was touching him.

Although he did not move, she felt, because her body was against his legs and her shoulders touched one of his arms, a quiver run through both of them.

She looked up into his face and this time their eyes met.

They were held spellbound by a magic that was inescapable, a magic which seemed to hold them as close and as entwined one with the other as if their lips actually met.

"Let me . . . stay with . . . you," Shimona whispered.

For a second she thought that his arms would go round her.

He did not move, but the lines on his face seemed to deepen and his eyes, which she hoped would somehow reflect the fire which she had seen in them before, only darkened.

Then in a voice that she had never heard him use, a voice that seemed to be strangled in his throat, the Duke said:

"I love you, God knows, I love you, but I cannot ask you to marry me!"

Chapter Seven

There was silence for a moment. Then Shimona dropped her eyes and said:

"Of course . . . I understand that you could not . . . marry the daughter of an . . . actor . . . but . . ."

"Good God, that is not the reason!" the Duke interrupted violently. "Did you really imagine that was why . . ."

He checked himself to say in a quieter voice:

"There is no man, whoever he might be, whatever his position in life, who would not be fortunate beyond words to be your husband."

Shimona looked at him and he saw the bewilderment in her face.

"I will explain everything to you," he said, "but go and sit in a chair. I cannot say what I have to say when you are so close to me."

Confused but obedient, Shimona rose from her knees and moved across the hearth to sit opposite him, her eyes on his face, her fingers linked together in her lap.

The Duke looked away from her into the fire, then he began:

"I am going to tell you about myself, not to make excuses for my behaviour, or for what I am, but simply because I want you to understand what I am trying to say to you."

Shimona waited and after a long pause he said:

"I do not suppose you heard of my father, but he was known as 'The Praying Duke.' He was sanctimonious, narrow-minded, and fanatical on the subject of sin."

144

Again there was a pause before the Duke went on:

"It is difficult for me to explain to you what it was like living with him after my mother died. I think, looking back into the past, he must have been unhinged and a little mad."

His voice was cynical as he continued:

"If anything was likely to put a child off religion it was living with my father. We had long family prayers in the morning with the whole Household there and the same thing at night, and everything that was amusing, interesting, or could in any way be construed as being a pleasure was forbidden."

"Why was he like that?" Shimona enquired.

"Heaven knows!" the Duke replied. "I only know that after my mother died, when I was seven, I lived in the nearest thing to a hell on earth."

Shimona made a little sound of commiseration and he went on:

"He was determined to bring me up in his own image and I was therefore not allowed the company of children of my own age, nor even to be looked after by a Nurse or Governess. I was in the hands of Tutors."

"It was much too young!" Shimona murmured.

"Of course it was!" the Duke answered. "And they were always elderly, erudite men who had not the slightest idea how to look after a child, let alone to interest his mind."

"It was cruel!"

"I realised how cruel when I was not allowed to go to school."

"You stayed at home?"

"With my Tutors always in attendance giving me lessons from the time I rose in the morning until last thing at night. I was allowed to ride, but not to play games."

"It must have been intolerable . . . and very lonely."

"I think the loneliness was the worst part," the Duke agreed. "I had no-one to talk to, no companion of any sort."

"How long did this go on?"

"Until I was eighteen."

"Oh, no! It cannot be true!"

"It was true!" the Duke said grimly. "So you can imagine that when my father died it was like coming out of prison."

He gave a short laugh.

"And like a prisoner who has been incarcerated for a lifetime, I found the world a strange place and had not the least understanding of it."

"What . . . happened?"

"Can you not guess the rest?" the Duke asked mockingly. "I came to London because I was now my own master. Society welcomed a wealthy Duke with open arms."

"It must . . . have been . . . enjoyable," Shimona said in a low voice.

"It was like coming out of the darkness into the light; but I had no power of discrimination, no standards by which to judge the people I met, nothing to guide me but a wild desire to make up for the time I had lost."

"I can . . . understand . . . that."

"I wanted to do everything that I had not been allowed to do in the past. I wanted to race my own horses, shoot, fence, fight, do all the things which every young man of my age had grown up doing."

The Duke's lips twisted a little cynically as he added:

"And naturally I wanted to meet women!"

Shimona pressed her fingers together. She felt a sudden stab of jealousy that was like a dagger piercing her heart.

"My father considered women were the invention of the Devil," the Duke went on. "So for me they had an attraction that drew me to them like a magnet."

Looking at his handsome face as he spoke, Shimona was well aware that women would have found him as attractive as he found them.

"Again I had no discrimination," he said, "and as

I started my life in the *Beau Monde* at Carlton House, the Prince of Wales's more disreputable friends were the ones who introduced me to the amusements with which they were all too familiar."

The Duke's voice was bitter as he said:

"You can imagine what happened. I was like a small boy let loose in a sweet-shop. I gorged myself greedily and in consequence earned very aptly the title I have been given."

His lips curled:

" 'His Disgrace'! I was quite proud of it! At least no-one would be likely to accuse me of being a 'Praying Duke'!"

He drew in his breath.

"Then I met you! When you came into the room at Ravenstone House I knew you were everything I always wanted and dreamt of and had never found."

"I . . . I too felt . . . something happened when we . . . met," Shimona murmured.

"We recognised each other," the Duke said. "We belonged, and there was no need for words."

He turned his face to look at her and she saw the pain in his eyes.

"When I kissed you I knew that after all there was a God and I believed in Him."

Shimona felt herself quiver as his words seemed to vibrate through her. Then he rose to his feet.

"But because you are everything that is pure and good," he said harshly, "and because I am what I have made myself, I still have enough decency left not to drag you down to my level."

He gave a deep sigh before he said very quietly:

"I shall love you all my life, and because I love you I shall send you away tomorrow to your grandparents where you will be safe. Perhaps one day you will find happiness with a man who is worthy of you."

Shimona was very still.

She understood so many things which had not been clear before.

She too had known a life without companions, she

too had known the loneliness of being kept apart from the world.

The Duke's prison had been a cruel and hard one. Hers had been comfortable and she had been encircled with love. But the enforced segregation had left its mark on both of them.

That was why she could understand exactly what he felt and also why he had behaved as he had.

She knew he was waiting for her to speak and she rose from the chair to stand beside him.

She had a feeling that he was tense.

Yet she knew by the firmness of his chin and the hard line of his lips that he meant what he said and that he was sending her away so that they would never see each other again.

She moved a little nearer to him and raised her face to his.

"I . . . I have . . . always heard," she said softly, "that if you . . . save someone's life . . . you are . . . responsible for them . . . forever!"

The Duke did not move, but she felt him stiffen.

"I . . . belong to you," Shimona went on. "I may be a nuisance . . . and an encumbrance . . . but I will not . . . leave you. I will follow you . . . and sit on the doorstep of Ravenstone House until you let me . . . in."

The Duke made a little sound that was half a laugh and half a sob, then he put out his arms to draw her against him.

"Do you know what you are saying?" he asked. "Do you really mean that you will stay with me? That you will marry me?"

"I love you!" Shimona answered. "I love you so . . . agonisingly that if you . . . send me away . . . I swear I shall die!"

"Oh—my darling . . ."

His voice broke as his arms tightened, and he was kissing her cheeks with hard, rough kisses as if he had lost control of his actions.

Their lips met . . . then there was the tenderness and gentleness that she had known before.

It was as if their two beings merged into each other and there was no longer any division, or any barrier between them. They became part of each other and once again there was the rapture and wonder of a Divine ecstasy.

They clung together as if they had passed through a tempestuous and dangerous sea, and had reached a harbour of safety where they need no longer be afraid.

Shimona felt as if her eyes were blinded with glory and her whole being vibrated to music which came from another sphere.

The Duke raised his head and looked down at her face. He had not known a woman could look so radiantly happy and at the same time so spiritual, and he felt as if he must kneel before her.

"I love you! My precious, my darling, my perfect little love!" he said brokenly.

Then with his face hidden against the softness of her neck he whispered:

"Help me to be—as you want me to be—because I could not bear to—disappoint you."

"I want you just as you have always been to me," Shimona replied, "kind and gentle . . . considerate and everything that is . . . fine and noble."

He raised his head.

"Do you mean that?"

"You know I mean it."

They looked into each other's eyes and the world seemed to stand still.

The Duke sat down in the arm-chair and drew Shimona into it beside him.

There was room for them both if he held her close in his arms.

"You must not . . . do too much," she said anxiously.

"You are not to worry about me."

"Can you expect me to do . . . anything else," she

asked, "when I thought I might have . . . lost you?"

There was a sob in her voice, then suddenly she hid her face against his shoulder.

"You are crying," the Duke said in a voice of consternation. "My precious darling, what has made you cry?"

"It is . . . because I am so . . . happy," Shimona sobbed. "I have been so . . . afraid that I would not be able to . . . stay with you . . . that you would not . . . want me."

"Not want you?" the Duke exclaimed. "Do you know what I have been through? Thinking about you, knowing that I must send you to your grandparents, and wondering how I could live through the rest of my life when you were no longer there."

"How could you . . . think of anything so . . . cruel?"

"I was thinking of you," he said. "I still am and I know that if I did what was right I would let you go."

"I have . . . already told you that I will not . . . let you do . . . that," Shimona replied, "and besides . . . I think you worry too much about your reputation. I do not know what terrible things you are supposed to have done. . . ."

"And I pray that you never will!" the Duke interposed.

Looking at the tears still wet on her cheeks, he asked:

"What were you going to say?"

"You . . . may not agree," Shimona said hesitatingly, "but I . . . thought that if we could . . . leave London for a little while and live in the country . . . in your house with the beautiful gardens, people would soon . . . stop talking about you and perhaps instead they would begin to talk about the . . . good things you are doing."

The Duke put his fingers under her chin and turned her face up to his.

"Is that what you would like?" he asked. "Tell me honestly. Would you be content with living in the country with me instead of going to Balls and Receptions and all the parties that you could enjoy in London?"

Shimona gave a little laugh.

"Since I have never been to any Balls and parties I certainly would not miss them! Besides, I would much rather be . . . alone with you than at the most splendid Ball that was ever given! I can imagine nothing more wonderful than to be in the country and be able to ride . . . and plan the gardens . . . so long as we do it . . . together."

The Duke pulled her closer against his heart.

"Together! That is the important word!" he said. "And there is in fact a lot for us to do at Ravenstone."

"What sort of things?" Shimona asked curiously.

"My father, because he disapproved of them, had every picture, however valuable or beautiful, which depicted women, especially those who were dressed, or should I say undressed, like goddesses, removed to the attics."

He smiled as he went on:

"With them went all the furniture that was carved with hearts or cupids, and a number of beds and sofas that he considered too comfortably luxurious to be anything but an invitation to indolence."

"It must have made your house very . . . austere."

"It is! That is why I have hardly lived there since I inherited the title," the Duke replied. "But we can restore it to its previous glory, put it back as it was when my grandfather rebuilt the house and brought treasures from Italy and France which are now heirlooms."

"I would love to do that."

"We will do it—together," the Duke answered.

"It sounds so . . . wonderful . . . so perfect!"

"And that is what you are!"

The Duke took his soft linen handkerchief and wiped the tears from her eyes, then he kissed them one after the other, and his lips lingered on the softness of her cheeks.

Then he pulled her even closer against him and found her mouth. He kissed her passionately, fiercely, possessively, and there was a fire burning in his eyes, but she was not afraid.

"I . . . love you!"

Shimona was not certain if she said the words aloud.

Her whole body vibrated with the wonder of him and the wild sensations he aroused in her.

They were no longer two people but one.

This, she thought, was what she had always wanted. This was what she had missed, a sense of belonging, of not being the "odd person out."

The Duke's hand was on her head, smoothing her hair.

"You are so beautiful!" he said hoarsely. "You will be the loveliest of all the Duchesses of Ravenstone."

"We will have our . . . portrait painted . . . together."

He laughed.

"Why not? And it will be entitled: 'Her Grace and His Dis . . .'"

Shimona put her fingers up to cover his lips.

"You are not to say it. That is all in the past . . . it is forgotten . . . and any wrong that resulted has been forgiven."

"How can you be sure of that?" the Duke enquired.

"There is something in the Bible," she answered, "about being 'purified by fire.' That is what you have been because you were so brave, because you saved me. We have started a new life . . . you and I . . . and never after today will we talk about the past."

She put her arm round his neck and drew his head a little closer to hers.

"I know that the consequences of what we will do . . . together will 'ripple out' and bring . . . blessings and happiness to many, many . . . people."

"My precious," the Duke said. "I love you! I adore you! I worship you!"

Then he was kissing her until again he swept her up into a boundless sky brilliant with stars where they were alone with their happiness and very near to God.

ABOUT THE AUTHOR

BARBARA CARTLAND, the celebrated romantic author, historian, playwright, lecturer, political speaker and television personality, has now written over 150 books. Miss Cartland has had a number of historical books published and several biographical ones, including that of her brother, Major Ronald Cartland, who was the first Member of Parliament to be killed in the War. This book had a Foreword by Sir Winston Churchill.

In private life, Barbara Cartland, who is a Dame of the Order of St. John of Jerusalem, has fought for better conditions and salaries for Midwives and Nurses. As President of the Royal College of Midwives (Hertfordshire Branch), she has been invested with the first Badge of Office ever given in Great Britain, which was subscribed to by the Midwives themselves. She has also championed the cause for old people and founded the first Romany Gypsy Camp in the world.

Barbara Cartland is deeply interested in Vitamin Therapy and is President of the British National Association for Health.